W9-CDH-721

The Case of the Dinosaur Birds

John R. Erickson

Illustrations by Gerald L. Holmes

Maverick Books, Inc.

MAVERICK BOOKS, INC.
Published by Maverick Books, Inc.
P.O. Box 549, Perryton, TX 79070
Phone: 806.435.7611
www.hankthecowdog.com

First published in the United States of America by Viking Children's Books and Puffin Books (simultaneously), members of Penguin Putnam Books for Young Readers, 2009.
Currently published by Maverick Books, Inc., 2012

1 3 5 7 9 10 8 6 4 2

Copyright © John R. Erickson, 2009
All rights reserved

LIBRARY OF CONGRESS CATALOGING-IN-PUBLICATION DATA
Erickson, John R., date.
The case of the dinosaur birds / John R. Erickson ; illustrations by Gerald L. Holmes.
p. cm. — (Hank the Cowdog ; #54)
Summary: Unaware that his nemesis Pete the Barncat is playing yet another prank on him, Hank the Cowdog, Head of Ranch Security, tries to save the world from "terradogtail" dinosaur birds armed with bacon-stealing laser tongs.
ISBN 978-1-59188-154-4 (paperback)
[1. Dogs—Fiction. 2. Ranch life—Texas—Fiction. 3. Pelicans—Fiction. 4. Texas—Fiction. 5. Humorous stories.] I. Holmes, Gerald L., ill. II. Title.
PZ7.E72556Cacn 2009
[Fic]—dc22
2008055399

Maverick Books, Inc. ISBN 978-1-59188-154-4

Hank the Cowdog® is a registered trademark of John R. Erickson.
Printed in the United States of America

Except in the United States of America, this book is sold subject to the condition that it shall not, by way of trade or otherwise, be lent, re-sold, hired out, or otherwise circulated without the publisher's prior consent in any form of binding or cover other than that in which it is published and without a similar condition including this condition being imposed on the subsequent purchaser.

The publisher does not have any control over and does not assume any responsibility for author or third-party Web sites or their content.

To Gene Edward Veith, Jr.,
scholar, author, teacher,
and friend

CONTENTS

We Assemble for a Scrap Event

It's me again, Hank the Cowdog. They were creatures like we'd never seen before. I had no idea who they were, where they'd come from, or what they were doing on my ranch; but I knew right away that they didn't belong to this world.

I also had reason to believe . . . Wait, hold everything, stop, halt. I'm not sure I should go public with this next piece of information. I mean, a guy should never put too much scary stuff at the first part of the story.

Why? The little children. You know where I stand on that issue. I don't mind giving the kids some excitement or even a little scare now and then, but I've got problems jumping into deep, scary stuff right away.

Oh, I know what you're thinking. You think you can handle the scary stuff because you've survived stories about the Silver Monster Bird, the Phantom in the Mirror, the Halloween Ghost, the Vampire Cat, and all the other monsters and goblins we've encountered on this ranch. Well, maybe you survived those deals, but don't let it cloud your judgment.

The truth is, you don't know what's coming in this story but I do, and I'm not ready to reveal any information about Prehistoric Dinosaur Birds, so don't even ask. In the first place, you wouldn't believe me; and in the second place, if you believed me, you'd be too scared to read the rest of the story.

So there's Ground Rule Number One: no mention of...Wait a second. Did I already...Okay, here's Ground Rule Number Two: In the event that I already flubbed up and broke Ground Rule Number One, you will disregard anything I might have said. You heard nothing about any kind of Unmentionable Something or Other.

That should take care of it, and now we're ready to mush on with the story.

It all began one morning. No, wait. It all began one evening; yes, I'm sure it was evening . . . or was it in the middle of the day? You know, I can't remember when it began and I don't care, because it began sometime and that's all we need to know. If it hadn't begun, we wouldn't be talking about it.

Now . . . what were we talking about? Hmmm. I know it was important, and it was right on the tip of my tock . . . the tip of my tongue, let us say. That's usually the best place to leave things, on the tick of your tock, because you can always come back later and find it. I mean, how can you lose something on the tang of your tongue?

It's impossible. On the other hand . . . you know, this is really embarrassing. All at once I've just . . . uh . . . drawn a blank. I have no idea what we were talking about, yet I have this feeling that it was very, very important.

I know what's causing this. Years of working around Drover has caused deposits of plaque to form around my brain cells. You know what plaque does to your teeth, right? Bad stuff. It causes tooth decay and root rot, so you can imagine what it does to brain cells. It causes us to babble and wander, so don't forget to brush those teeth twice a day and use dental floss.

And don't swallow the floss. Floss is string, and nobody needs dental string in his gizzard. Ask a guy who knows. I once swallowed a piece of string that had a fishhook tied to it and . . .

How did we get on the subject of string and

fishhooks? This is crazy. You know, before I began working with Drover, I had no trouble carrying on a normal conversation or following a train of thought, but now . . .

Wait! I just remembered. Forget about fishhooks. It was morning on the ranch, and you know what big event happens around here in the morning. Here's a hint. It begins with "Scrap" and ends with "Time."

Scrap Time. Did you get the right answer? Good. Yes, in this outfit a normal day begins around eight o'clock when our Beloved Ranch Wife, Sally May, comes out the back door with a plate of luscious breakfast scraps.

Even on a bad day, Scrap Time brings meaning and focus into a dog's life. It gives us a break from the crushing routine of running the ranch's Security Division twenty-four hours a day, and we're talking about crinimal investigations, barking at the mailman, Chicken House Patrol, Monster Watch, and all the other things we do around here.

Heavy responsibility, and it's very important that we have a few precious moments every morning to, you know, keep ourselves pumped and excited about Life, work, and all the so-forth.

At an ordinary Scrap Event, we can expect a few morsels of scrambled eggs and several pieces of burned toast. But on a *good* day, we'll get egg scraps, burned toast, plus five or six fatty, juicy ends of bacon.

You know where I stand on the Issue of Bacon. I love the stuff, absolutely love it, and that's why Drover and I always try to arrive early for Scrap Events. We want to be first in line so that we can protect our bacon scraps from the local cat.

Have we discussed cats? Maybe not. I don't like 'em, and I especially don't like the one we're stuck with on this ranch. Pete. He's a sneak and a slacker, and he spends all his waking hours lusting for fatty, juicy ends of bacon.

So do I, but it's different when a dog does it. Cats are pure gluttons, see, whereas your higher rank of dogs are more refined. We play by the Rules of Good Behavior. We wait our turn in line. Cats don't even know that rules exist, and given the slightest opportunity, they will cheat every time.

Show me a cat and I'll show you a cheater.

That's why it's so important that we dogs arrive early at our Scrap Events. It gives us an opportunity to set the proper tone: rules and manners; no scuffling, hissing, pushing, shoving, or bickering over the scraps.

Pretty impressive, huh? You bet. I mean, food

is important, but we can't allow it to rule our lives. If a guy wins all the scraps but loses his poise in the process...well, what's the point? He's no better than your average cat.

And speaking of cats, when Drover and I arrived at the yard gate—five minutes early, mind you—we found that the cat was already there, sitting with his tail wrapped around his backside, beaming a gluttonous look toward the house, and purring like a little . . . something. Like a greedy little motorboat.

When he heard us coming, he turned and flashed his usual smirk. "My, my, it's Hankie the Wonder Dog...and you're late."

I thundered up to him. "We're not late, Kitty. We came five minutes early so that we could be first in line."

"Well, darn the luck. I guess it didn't work."

I stuck my nose in his face. "I guess it *did* work, you little pestilence."

"No, no, Hankie. As you can see, I'm first in line." He batted his eyes and snickered. "And you're not."

"Oh yeah? Well, here's some bad news. The line you started was the Cheater's Line. We're starting a new line, the Line of Good Behavior. Go to the back of the line."

"But Hankie, I won fair and square by coming earlier than you. Tee hee."

"Right, and that's cheating."

"That's the way the game is played, Hankie."

"That's the way the cheater's game is played. This is a new game, and we're going to play by the rules."

He licked his paw with a long stroke of his tongue. "Oh, really? What rules are we talking about?"

"The Rules of Justice, Pete, and Rule Number One is that cats always go last. Go to the rear. Move!"

His gaze drifted around. "You know, Hankie, this won't work. It never works because . . ." He fluttered his eyelids. ". . . Sally May brings the scraps, and I'm her special pet. You know what will happen if you make a scene."

I heard a growl rumbling in the darkness of my throat. "Pete, you're despicable."

"I know, and sometimes it really bothers me. But not today. Tee hee."

For a moment of heartbeats, my finger twitched on the Launch Button. It would have been so easy to dive right into the middle of the little snot and give him the thrashing he so richly deserved. But at the last second, I canceled the launch and took a step backward. I mean, one of us had to show some maturity, right?

"Okay, Pete, just this once I'm going to let it slide."

"I thought you'd see it that way."

"And I hope you get indigestion."

At that very moment, the back door opened and out stepped . . . holy smokes, I couldn't believe my good fortune . . . out stepped my very best pal in the whole world.

Little Alfred!

Do you see the meaning of this? Heh heh. I did, and so did Kitty-Kitty.

Strange Birds in the Sky

See, here's the deal. Little Alfred was a fine young man, fair and honest, and best of all he had no history of pampering cats, unlike his mother who...

I would be the last dog in the world to say a critical word about the Lady of the House, but let's be frank. There had been times in our long and stormy relationship when I had looked into Sally May's eyes and had gotten the feeling that, well, she wasn't fond of dogs.

Or was it just me? Surely not. No, our troubled relationship grew out of the fact that she had a weakness for cats, and that's a very sad state of affairs. People who don't understand the true crooked nature of cats . . . Maybe we'd better leave this subject alone.

The point is that Little Alfred wasn't as likely to fall for Pete's trickery; and when Kitty saw him coming out the door with the plate of scraps, that insolent smirk on his face dropped dead. He swung his eyes around to me and gave me a hateful glare.

I was beside myself with joy that the Cause of Justice had been served. "Hey, Pete, what do you say now, huh? Ha ha ha! Where's Sally May?"

"This isn't funny, Hankie."

"Of course it is. It's hilarious. Go to the back of the line." He didn't move, so I did what any normal dog would have done. I gave him a loud burst of self-righteous barking. We call it our Train Horns Application.

BWONK!

Heh heh. I love doing that, especially when Sally May isn't around with her broom. Kitty responded just as I had hoped. He jumped three feet in the air, turned wrong side out, hissed, spit, shrieked, and humped his back. Okay, maybe he landed one lucky punch with his claws, but I hardly even . . .

Actually, it stung like crazy, but never mind. The important thing is that a spoiled, pampered, rinky-dink little ranch cat had been humbled and the Cause of Justice had been served.

Kitty gave me the Cobra Eye and began slinking toward the rear of the line, the very spot in Life where every cat belongs. "Very well, Hankie, but things have a way of coming back around."

"Do they? That's great. This time I gave you Train Horns, and next time I'll show you Ocean Liner Horn. I guarantee you won't like it."

At that point, I whirled away from the sulking cat and prepared myself for the Scrap Event. You'll be impressed by this. See, a lot of your ordinary dogs would have gone into a wild celebration—jumping around, thrashing their tails, barking, drooling, making a big scene.

Not me. I made a special effort to control my savage instincts because . . . well, when you know that you've won the big game, you don't need to gloat. Gloating can be a lot of fun, but it's only icicles on the cake. Winning is enough.

And so it was that I turned to the control panel in my mind and began flipping switches.

Leaps and Dives: OFF.

Wild, Exuberant Swings on the Tail Section: OFF.

Dripping Tongue: OFF.

Eyes Blazing with Food Lust: OFF.

As the boy came down the sidewalk, I sat on the ground beside the yard gate, first in line, a perfect doggly gentleman waiting to receive his scrap award.

He gave me a smile. "Hi, Hankie. You want some skwaps?"

I was trembling with excitement but didn't let it show. He opened the gate and held the plate under my . . . BACON! Holy smokes, I had won the lottery! Six or seven fatty, juicy, fragrant ends of bacon!

Yes, I wanted scraps, but I would be a gentleman about it. I was first in line, so there was no need to behave like a slob. I held tight to my emotions and beamed him a look that said "Just any morsel will be fine."

He was impressed. He should have been. He gave me a pat on the head and looked at the food line, which consisted of me first, Drover second, and Kitty O'Glutton on the tail end. Tee hee.

"Okay, y'all, make a line along the fence, and don't eat till I give the signal."

Yes sir! I was already in the right place, so Drover and Kitty pushed and shoved to get the slots to my right. We ended up with a new line: me on the left, Drover in the middle, and Pete on the far right. We all turned our eyes toward the boy.

He gave his head a nod. "That's good. Now, since Hankie was first in line, I'm going to give him the bacon." He scraped the bacon onto the ground in front of me.

To my right, I heard odd noises. Drover let out a moan, and Pete made the sound cats make when they're very unhappy—the yowl that reminds you of a police siren. He was hating this; and while I didn't wish to be overbearing, I allowed myself to whisper, "Something wrong, Pete? Talk to me, pal. Hey, if you've got any gripes about the service, call the manager. Raise a fuss, file a complaint, don't be bashful."

The look he gave me would have scalded the feathers off of thirteen chickens. He was mad, fellers, but there wasn't a thing he could do about it. Hee hee.

Alfred moved on down the line. He scraped some egg scraps in front of Drover and moved on to Pete. "Welp, alls that's left is a biscuit, Pete. You want a biscuit?" Pete let loose a pitiful whine. Alfred shrugged. "I don't think Hankie will share his bacon."

Exactly right. Hankie would NOT share his bacon with the little moocher. If Kitty wanted bacon, he should have come early and waited in line like the rest of us.

Well, the scraps had been distributed, and all that remained was for Alfred to give us the signal to start gobbling...uh, eating, let us say. My whole body quivered with antsippitation as he lifted his right hand into the air.

"Ready?"

I froze, waiting for his hand to come down. It didn't. Instead, his gaze rose up to the sky, and he said, "Wowee, look at those birds!"

A voice in my mind cried out, "Wowee, forget the birds; let's eat!"

But his gaze was locked on the sky. "They look like pterodoctyles—dinosaur birds!" He dashed back to the porch. "Mom, come look!"

Rats. Breakfast had been put on hold. So, with nothing better to do, I lifted my gaze and studied the objects in the sky. At first I thought they were buzzards, large birds that move through the air with slow flaps of their wings.

But a closer inspection revealed something else. They had long necks that stuck out in front and long skinny legs that stuck out behind, and... their beaks! My goodness, they had incredibly long beaks.

These were not buzzards or hawks or owls or any other kind of bird that lived on my ranch. I had never seen a...what had Alfred called them?

Terra-dog-tails? I had never seen a Terradogtail, but Alfred had several books on dinosaurs, and by George, if the boy said those were Terradogtail Dinosaur Birds, maybe they were.

Sally May came out the door, wiping her hands on her apron. She looked up into the sky. "Well, my stars, I've never seen such a thing."

"They're pterodoctyles, Mom, I've seen 'em in pictures!"

She laughed. "Well, I think pterodactyls are extinct." She noticed us waiting at the yard fence. "Sweetie, your little friends are waiting for their breakfast. You'd better let them eat. When Daddy gets home, we'll ask him about the birds."

Right. Forget the birds.

Alfred came back to the gate. He lifted his right arm. "Ready?" Yes, yes, we'd been ready for hours. "Okay!" His arm swooped downward, giving us the long-awaited signal to dive in and...

Huh?

MY BACON WAS GONE!

I whirled around to the right and faced Drover, who was gobbling his scrambled eggs. "Drover, only seconds ago I had seven fatty ends of bacon right here in front of me. If you stole my bacon..."

"It wasn't me. I've got eggs." In saying this, he

splattered my face with several fragments of half-chewed egg.

"Yes, and you just spewed egg bits into my face!"

"Well, you made me talk with my mouth full."

"And you just did it again!"

"Sorry."

"Greedy pig! Stop spitting egg on me!"

"Well, leave me alone and let me eat."

"This will go into my report!"

I wiped the egg off my face, whirled around to my left, and beamed a murderous glare at the cat. He was trying to chew his biscuit and seemed to be having some trouble. On another occasion, I would have paused to enjoy the spectacle of him wrestling with a hard biscuit, but not now.

"Pete, someone has stolen my bacon, and I'm putting the entire ranch under Lockdown. Drop the biscuit and take three steps back. Move!"

To my astonishment, the cat did as he was told. I mean, this might have been the first time in history that a cat had ever followed an order. Obviously, the little creep had seen the fury in my eyes and had decided to keep his mouth shut. Good idea. I mean, the cat had become a prime suspect in this case.

When he backed away from the fence, I moved

in and began sweeping the entire area with Snifforadar. If Pete had pulled the job, surely Snifforadar would pick up traces of bacon scent. I did a thorough sweep of the ground but came up with nothing but readings of cat and biscuit.

I entered all the information into Data Control and waited for it to come up with a solution. A moment later, a message flashed across the screen of my mind. *"You've got a flea biting your left ear."*

Ouch! It was true. I'd been so busy with other things, I hadn't even noticed. Right then and there, I put the investigation on hold, dropped my bottom side to the ground, and began hacking my left ear with powerful sweeps of my left hind foot.

The good news was that I vaporized the flea. The bad news was that I still had no idea who had robbed my bacon. And that was bad news.

My Bacon Is Burgled

I leaped to my feet and gave myself a vigorous shake. The Anti-Flea Procedure had worked to perfection, and now it was time to solve the Case of the Burgled Bacon. Unfortunately, I had no leads in the case and would have to depend on luck to pull me through.

Kitty was staring at me. I had his full attention. I marched over to the biscuit, which was still lying on the ground near the fence. "What's this?"

"My pitiful little breakfast, Hankie."

"Then why haven't you eaten it? Is it possible that you were stealing my bacon?"

"No, Hankie, cats are delicate eaters. Unlike certain dogs I could name, we don't gorge and gobble our food."

"Stick with the facts, Pete. I don't care about your opinions. It makes me suspicious that you've hardly made a dent in the biscuit. Explain."

"Well, Hankie, it was stale and crusty and hard to chew."

"Ha. You expect me to believe that?" I lowered my nose and gave the biscuit a sniffing. "Hey, this smells pretty good. I'll have to take it in for evidence." I swept it up in my mouth and began chewing. "Okay, go on with your..."

CRUNCH. CRACK.

By George, it *was* kind of hard to chew... very hard to chew ... Good grief, it was as hard as a rock, and even my powerful jaws had trouble...

You know, when you crush a stale biscuit, what you end up with is a mouthful of sharp little crumbs; and when you pull the Flush Lever and try to sweep the crumbs down your guzzle, they can...

COUGH, HARK, WHEEZE.

. . . Sometimes they get caught in your . . . HARK, HACK . . . breathing pipe. And that's exactly what happened here. A hateful little biscuit crumb lodged in my... HONK, HARK... breathing apparatus and caused me to choke. It took me a whole minute to work myself through this episode, and by then my eyes were watering and my voice had been reduced to a croak.

I turned to the cat. "Okay, maybe you were right about the biscuit."

"I always tell the truth, Hankie."

"You rarely tell the truth, Pete, yet you just told the truth. That worries me. Why, all of a sudden, did you give me an honest answer?"

"Well, Hankie, I want to help you solve your case."

I stared into his big moon eyes. "You want to help me catch the Bacon Burglar? Pete, forgive me if I seem suspicious, but why would you do that?"

He drummed his claws on the ground. "Well, Hankie, I want to get on with my life, and I know you won't give me a minute's peace until you catch the thief."

My first impulse was to laugh out loud, but something told me to follow up on this. "Keep talking. Are you saying that you have some information?"

"I do, Hankie. While you were looking at the birds, I saw what happened to your bacon."

I moved closer. "You did? By any chance, was it Drover?"

"Not Drover. He was busy with his eggs."

"That checks out. We're down to one suspect. You."

"Not me, Hankie. I was trying to chew my biscuit, remember?"

I cut my eyes from side to side. "Okay, but that means we're out of suspects."

His eyes drifted around, and a little smile twitched at his mouth. "It's so obvious, you don't see it. What drew your attention away from the bacon?"

"Birds. I was looking at a couple of odd-looking birds in the sky."

"They were more than odd-looking birds, Hankie." He dropped his voice to a spooky whisper and widened his eyes. "They were *dinosaur birds* from another dimension of time and space! I guess you know about dinosaur birds."

His voice and manner sent a chill down my spine. I took a step backward. "Of course I do. What's your point?"

Pete glanced over each shoulder and moved closer. "Surely you know that they're equipped with an Ultra Guzzonic Bacon Beacon."

"What? Ultra Guzzonic . . . is this some kind of joke?"

He shrugged. "If you think so, Hankie. I was just trying to help."

"Yeah? Well, the day I need help from a cat is the day I'll eat turnips for breakfast. Run along and chase your tail."

I whirled around and stormed away. What a pathetic little creep! Ultra Guzzonic Bacon Beacon! Ha. It was pure garbage, exactly what you'd expect to hear from . . . I stopped and, uh, found myself easing back toward the cat.

"Hey Pete, let's put the cards on the table. My knowledge of dinosaurs is a little rusty. To be honest, I don't know beans about them. Could you . . . Pete, it's very hard for me to say this."

"I know it is, Hankie. You can't bring yourself to ask me for help."

"Right. I mean, a guy in my position has to guard his reputation, know what I mean?"

"I understand, Hankie. What do you want to know?"

I shot a glance at Drover, just to be sure he wasn't listening. "Tell me more about the Bacon Beacon."

Pete rolled over on his back and began playing with his tail. "Well, Hankie, dinosaur birds are able to generate a powerful Guzzonic Beacon. It can locate every piece of bacon in a wide area and even *pull it up into the sky*."

"So, you're saying . . . you actually think those birds stole my bacon?"

He nodded. "I saw it rising off the ground, and then . . . poof . . . it zoomed off inside the Guzzonic Beam, straight to those birds. You didn't notice?"

"I didn't say that. I, uh, saw something, but it was just a blur."

"That was your bacon, Hankie, going bye-bye."

I gave this some heavy thought. "Okay, but why dinosaurs, Pete? Where did they come from? Why are they here?"

He slapped at his tail. "It's very mysterious, Hankie. Scientists thought they went extinct, but it appears that at least two of them survived."

"Wait! Hold it right there." I began pacing, as I often do when my mind shifts into a higher gear. "This is beginning to add up. Egg-stinct, Pete. Don't you get it? Bacon, eggs? There's our missing piece of the puzzle. Dinosaur birds live on bacon and eggs, and when they can't find them in the wild, they steal them from dogs!"

Pete made a peculiar snorting sound. "Pffft. My, my, Hankie, I never would have thought of that."

I whirled around and faced him with a triumphant smile. "Just follow the clues, Pete. Those birds have been flying around for years, using their Bacon Beacons to search for food, and today they found it."

"Pfftt! Yes, they did, Hankie, hee hee."

"And it was my bad luck that they came on the very day that I won the breakfast lottery."

"Hankie, I think you must be, hee hee, a genius!"

"Well, I wouldn't go that far, but . . . Hey, they didn't make me Head of Ranch Security just for my good looks." I noticed that the cat was wheezing and crawling on his belly. "Are you sick?"

"Oh no, it's nothing." Suddenly he cut loose with a squeaky little burp. "Oops, sorry. I guess I ate too fast. The biscuit."

"Right. That was a bad biscuit." My nose shot up in the air and began drawing in air samples. "Hmm, that's odd. All at once I'm picking up the scent of bacon. Do you smell it?"

The poor cat let out a screech of... something... pain, I guess. I mean, it sounded a lot like a screech of laughter, but surely not, and he began crawling away. "It's a residual cloud of bacon vapor . . . hee hee . . . from the Bacon Beacon . . . hee haw, HARK, HACK... Excuse me, I have to be going!"

He crawled away, moaning and groaning. Gee, this was kind of sad. I mean, nobody would be inclined to stop the world over a sick cat, but still.

BURP

. . I kind of hated to see the little creep . . . Pete, that is . . . I kind of hated to see Pete feeling so poorly. I had to admit that he'd given me some pretty important information on the Dinosaur Case.

Oh well. One cat in, one cat out, life goes on. I marched over to Drover, who had gorged himself on scrambled eggs and was now licking the dirt. "That's enough, Drover. Stop making a spectacle of yourself. Someone might be watching."

"Well, there's still a taste left on the ground. Boy, those were some great eggs."

"Yes, and while you were making a pig of yourself, two dinosaur birds flew over and stole my bacon."

He stared at me. "That's a joke, right?"

I showed him some fangs. "Does it look like I'm joking?"

"No, but I saw who stole . . ."

"You saw nothing. Your head was down, your eyes were down, your brain was down, and you were eating like a greedy pig. Furthermore, you spat particles of egg in my face, not once but twice."

"Yeah, but . . ."

"It will go into my report. Now, I'm going down to the office to catch up on some paperwork. Be on the alert for two strange-looking birds. If you see them, I want to be informed at once."

“Yeah, but I can tell you . . .”

I marched away and left him to enjoy his own boring company. Actually, I didn’t care if he wanted to lick dirt as long as I wasn’t around. If we’d been seen together, someone might have thought we were friends.

Everything You Want to Know About Dinosaurs

Leaving Drover to lick dirt and do other things too silly to contemplate, I made my way down to the Security Division's Vast Office Complex and rode the elevator up to my office on the twelfth floor.

There, I opened the drapes and gazed out the huge windows at the scene that stretched before me: skyscrapers, tugboats on the river, hundreds of taxi cabs moving up Broadway like little yellow bugs. Down there, it was a normal day. Up where I worked, the day was anything but normal.

I had gotten myself involved in a case concerning the appearance of a couple of Terradogtail

Dinosaur Birds, a type of rare creature that had never been observed on my ranch until today. So far we could link them to only one crime, the Bacon Theft; but I had an uneasy feeling that if they hung around the ranch, it could lead to a whole spree of crinimal activity.

In Security Work, it's very important to know the other guy: where he came from, where he sleeps at night, what he eats, what he thinks about in quiet moments. I knew almost nothing about Terradogtail Dinosaur Birds other than the few shreds of information I had managed to pry out of the cat. Shall we go over the Clue List? Might as well.

Clue Number One: Dinosaur birds can fly. Maybe that seems obvious because, well, most birds can fly, so let's move along to the next clue.

Clue Number Two: Through our network of undercover agents, we had learned that dinosaur birds are equipped with some very high-tech equipment that can locate tiny fragments of bacon, and do it from hundreds of feet in the air. We had no systems that could knock out their Bacon Radar.

Clue Number Three: The fact that these dino birds were running Bacon Radar was worrisome enough. Even more frightening was that they also had Laser Tongs that could snatch precious scraps off the ground, which meant that our entire inventory of morning scraps was now in danger of being compromised.

Clue Number Four: We had an eyewitness report of their first hit on our Scrap Inventory, and we knew that they could strike without warning, making no sound and leaving no tracks behind. That was scary.

Clue Number Five: We didn't actually have a Clue Number Five, so we'll move along.

As you can see, we were going into this case without much hard information on the bad guys. It was time to bring in Data Control and learn everything we could possibly learn about dinosaurs, and that's what I did. For the next two or three hours, I called up one classified document after another and educated myself on the subject of dinosaurs.

It's too bad we don't have time to look at some of those reports. I mean, you talk about interesting! That stuff was fascinating and I really wish . . . Do we have time to take a peek at the Dinosaur Files? No, but by George, we're going to *make* time. You'll want to hear this, but don't forget that it's Highly Classified. Not a word to anyone.

Here we go—everything everyone has ever

wanted to know about dinosaurs. But I must warn you that we'll be using a bunch of heavy-duty scientific words. Don't let the big words scare you. Take 'em one at a time and remember that most dinosaur words end with "-saurus."

Okay, let's start with the fact that there's more than one kind of dinosaur. There were a whole bunch of them. Some were big, some were little, and some were in between. Some walked upright on two legs; others walked downright on four legs or five legs or seven legs. The famous seven-legged dinosaur was called the *Sevenosaurus*.

Some of these creatures ate only vegetables (the *Carrotosaurus* and the *Spinachosaurus*). Some ate nothing but meat (the *Beefiosaurus* and the *Porkiosaurus*), and there was even one that ate nothing but sweets, the *Cookieosaurus*.

Other dinosaurs got their names from their appearance. *Lumposaurus* had knots on its back. *Jumposaurus* could leap over trees and mountains. *Rumposaurus* had a big tail. *Bumposaurus* was clumsy and ran into things. *Stumposaurus* was short and squatty. *Gumposaurus* was kind of dumb. *Trunkosaurus* had a long nose, like an elephant, and *Junkosaurus* collected bones and cans, like a pack rat.

The very largest of the dinosaurs (you've

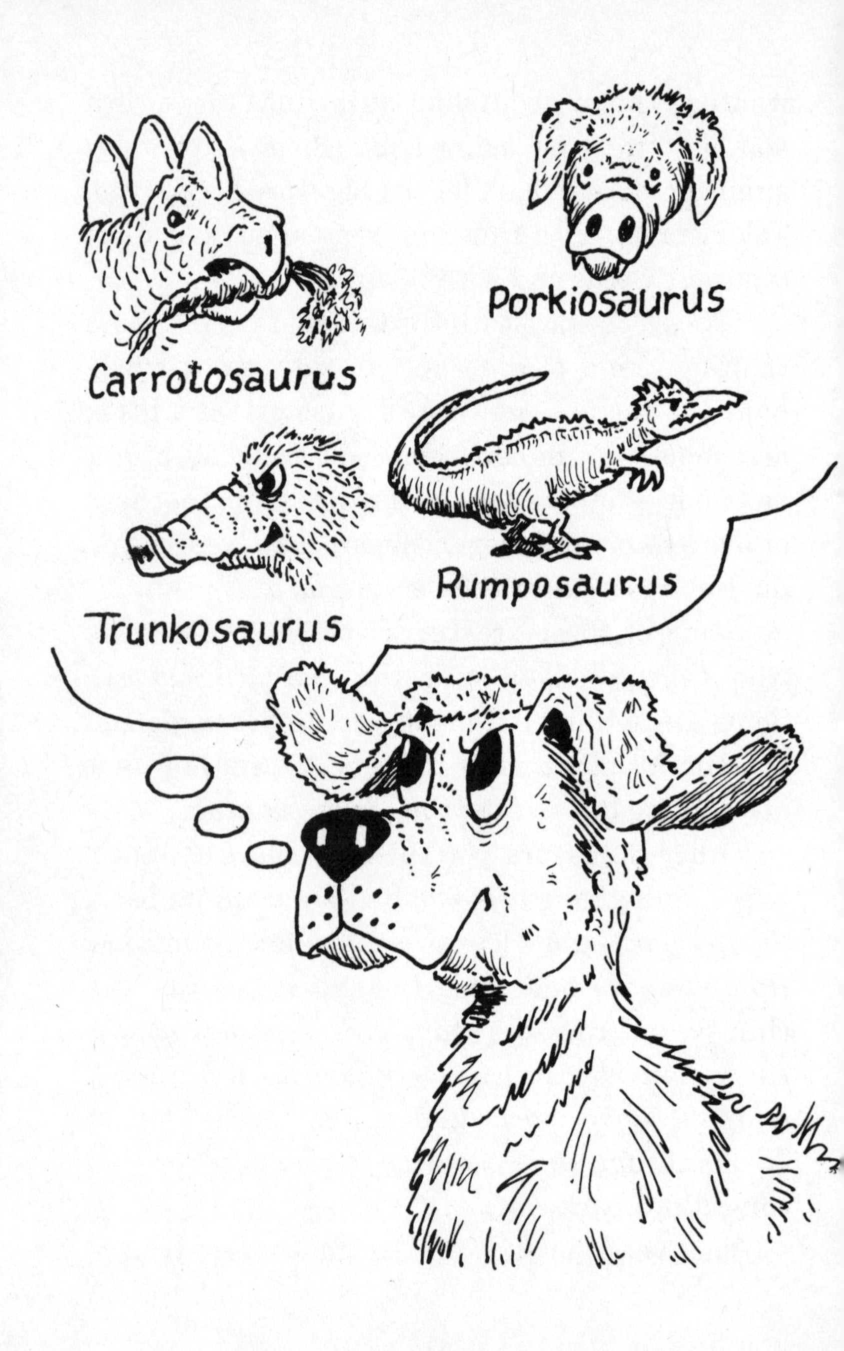
Carrotosaurus
Porkiosaurus
Trunkosaurus
Rumposaurus

probably seen pictures of this one: long neck and long tail) was called *Jumbo Eekosaurus*. Once again, the name tells us about the appearance of the beast: “Jumbo” (huge), “Eek” (scary), and “Saurus” (dinosaur). Put ’em all together and you get “huge scary dinosaur.”

Heh heh. Pretty impressive, huh? You bet. Most of your ordinary mutts would get lost in this kind of heavy-duty discussion of words and scientific so-forth. I mean, let’s face it. Most dogs know about three words: “eat,” “sleep,” and “duh.”

Me? I get a kick out of messing with the big, dangerous words and helping the children learn about the world we live in.

Anyway, that pretty muchly covers the whole subject of . . . no, wait, there’s one more thing we need to say about dinosaurs. If all dinosaurs have “-saurus” in their names, why are dinosaur birds called TERRADOGTAILS?

They should be called *Birdosaurus* or *Chirposaurus* or something that would make you think “dinosaur bird.” But that’s not the way it turned out. Why? Great question, and you know what?

I have no idea, so let’s skip it.

It’s kind of amazing that a dog would know so much about this stuff, isn’t it? I’ve already said that, but it's worth repeating repeating. Any dog who goes into this line of work must be a jackhammer of all trades. Some days we jack more than we hammer, and some days we hammer more than we jack; but the education never stops. When you spend your days and nights matching wits with crinimals and spies and exotic dinosaur birds, you have to stay on top of your business.

Anyway, there I was at my desk, studying all the so-forth, when a total stranger burst out of the elevator and came sprinting into the office. "Hank, you'd better wake up! I just saw those birds, and you need to come take a look."

When a total stranger bursts into your office and calls you by name, it makes you wonder how much of a total stranger he could be. I mean, that's pretty strange. Stranger still was the fact that the stranger had told me to *wake up*. Put those two clues together and you get an interesting profile: The guy thought he knew me, and he thought I was asleep.

Me, asleep during the day, during office hours? Ha ha. I don't need to tell you how ridiculous that was, but I'll say it anyway, just for the record. It was ridiculous. Outrageous. The Head of Ranch Security does not fall asleep at his desk on the twelfth floor of the Security Division's Vast Office Complex. Period.

Or, to come at it from a slightly different angle . . . okay, maybe I had dozed off, but who wouldn't have dozed off? Hey, I'd been putting in eighteen hours a day and burning the candle with both lightbulbs. I was worn to a frazzle, exhausted by the heavy responsibility of running my ranch, and maybe I had slipped off into a light doze, and I'm not ashamed to admit it.

Anyway, this guy came bursting into the office, and there he stood right in front of me. Description: big guy, huge, five feet tall at the shoulders; massive head; teeth like a shark; wicked red eyes that blinked on and off like a neon sign. For several long moments, we stared into our respective eyes (I stared into his, he stared into mine), and an eerie silence grew between us like . . . well, like an eerie silence.

I rose from my chair, spread my right paw into a karate-chopping device, and said, "Whenever the spinach leaves, the sprouts go on forever!"

This must have really rocked him back on his axles, and all he could say was, "What?"

So I repeated my statement, only louder this time. "Utility poles will never be toothpicks, regardless of the whickerbills!" I blinked my eyes and looked closer at the stranger. "Who are you? Have we met before?"

"Yeah, we meet about a hundred times every day. I'm Drover."

I narrowed my eyes and studied him closer. "Whose driver?"

He grinned. "No, I'm Drover, plain old Drover."

"Okay, maybe you're Drover now, but who were you when you walked into this office? The dog I saw was huge, and he had blinking red eyes."

"Nope, it was me all along. I guess you were asleep."

I strolled over to the door and peeked out into the hall, just to be sure that we weren't being eavesdropped on by a cat or an enemy spy. Only then did I return to his side and whisper, "Drivel, I'm going to ignore what you said about me being asleep. If I were to put that into my report, it would come back to honk you."

"Yeah, but my name's Drover."

"Please stop telling me your name. I know your name."

"What is it?"

"Drivel."

"No. Drover, Drover with a *D*."

"Oh, you think I can't spell? Is that what you're saying?"

"Well . . . I think you're still asleep."

"Who sent you? I must know. It could send this case into an entirely different direction."

He gave his head a shake. "Well, I was Drover when I walked in, and I'm still Drover and nobody sent me."

I studied his face again, more deeply this time. "Wait, hold everything. *You're Drover!*"

Holy smokes, it was my assistant, and I had just caught him sneaking around in my office. Had he parachuted onto the roof of our building and broken in through one of the sealed glass windows? Had he been stealing top-secret information out of our files?

I didn't know, but I had to find out. Don't forget the wise old saying . . . I can't remember the wise old saying, so skip it. The point is that I had to find out what was going on in my own office.

I began pacing, as I often do when we have fog at the top of the mountain. "All right, let's go over this one more time. How did you get into my office?"

"Well, I just walked in."

"Ah! So this didn't involve helicopters or commando units? Is that your version of events?"

"Yep."

"Okay, you say you 'walked in.' Does that mean you used your own legs?"

"Yeah, all four of 'em. Sometimes I limp, but my bad leg's been holding up pretty well."

My eyes prowled around the office as I put these two clues together: bad leg and limp. "Okay, this is matching up with our profiles. You really *are* Drover."

"Oh good. That's what I thought."

"But why were you trying to use a false identity? Never mind. What are you doing in my office?"

"Well . . . I came to tell you something."

I stopped pacing and gave him a cunning squint. "You weren't trying to break into our files?"

"We don't have any files."

"Hmmm. Great point." I paced a few steps away from him. "Very well, if you came to tell me something, maybe you should tell me."

Keep reading. This next part is pretty amazing.

Drover's Shocking Report

Drover had come bursting into my office, remember? And he'd said he had something important to tell me. After a moment of silence, I said, "Go on with your story. You said something about spinach leaves."

He gave his head a weary shake. "You've got me so messed up, I can't remember what I'm doing here."

"Oh, you're going to blame me? Drover, you've been messed up for years. I should have said something about it a long time ago, but I didn't want to hurt your feelings."

"Thanks."

"You're welcome. When did you first notice the spinach leaves?"

"Yesterday... today... I don't know."

"Were they in the garden?"

"I guess. I don't care."

I glared at the runt. "If you don't care, then why did you come blundering into my office, screeching about spinach? How can a dog get any work done around here?"

"You were asleep."

"I was not..." My gaze drifted around. "Drover, I think I've just figured it out. I must have been asleep. I guess the pressure finally wore me down." I pointed to a chair. "Here, sit down and let's chat. It's not often that I have a moment to chat with the men." He sat down. I sat down. "Tell me about the toothpicks."

"Well, they're little sticks of wood."

"Yes? Go on."

"Well... dogs never use 'em."

"Then why did you bring it up?"

"I didn't bring it up. You did, toothpicks and spinach leaves."

"What? You mean..." My gaze moved around the room. I saw the gas tanks, two gunnysack beds, and Drover. After a long moment of silence, I cleared my throat. "Drover, there's something I must tell you."

"Yeah, and I had something to tell you, if I can remember what it was."

"I have seniority so I'll speak first." I leaned toward him and spoke in a hushed tone. "Drover, this conversation we've just had . . . in some ways, I feel that it lacked . . . uh . . . clarity."

"Yeah, and clarity begins at home."

"Exactly, and home is where the heart attack is." There was a long moment of silence. "Drover, I suggest we forget that we ever had this conversation. The world must never be told what goes on inside these walls."

He glanced around. "We don't even have any walls."

"Exactly my point. If our people ever suspected that their dogs carried on loony conversations behind walls that don't exist, we could lose our jobs. Now, tell me why you came bursting into my office."

Drover gave me a blank stare. "Well, let me think here." He wadded up his face into a knot of flesh and hair, and rolled one eye around. It appeared that he had entered into a moment of deep concentration. At last he said, "Oh yeah, now I remember. I saw two big birds out in the pasture."

"Birds? I'm not interested in birds."

"Yeah, but you told me to watch for 'em. They're huge and have long skinny legs."

"Buzzards, Drover, probably Wallace and Junior, and I'm still not interested."

He dropped his voice. "They're not buzzards. I think they might be those Dinosaur Birds."

I stared at the runt. "The dinosaur birds! Why wasn't I informed of this?"

"Well, I tried, but you..."

I leaped out of my chair... Okay, I leaped out of my gunnysack bed. Our ranch is such a fleabag outfit, a stinking gunnysack is all the furniture we have in our office. You'd think... oh well.

"All right, son, let's check it out."

Drover led the way and I followed him past the garden, past the corrals, past Emerald Pond, up the hill, past the machine shed, and out into the home pasture. I figured this would be a dry run. Most likely he'd seen a couple of chickens or buzzards or maybe killdeers. Drover has a wild imagination, you know, and his reports can't be trusted.

After we had passed the machine shed, he stopped and pointed at something in the distance. "There, see?"

It appeared that he was pointing toward something... two somethings that wore feathers and stood on long skinny legs... and, my goodness, they weren't buzzards, chickens, or killdeers. I squinted my eyes and looked closer and noticed... their beaks were ENORMOUS, I mean, almost as long as their bodies!

Huh?

Holy smokes, he was right. Terradogtail Dinosaur Birds, two of 'em.

Suddenly I felt the hair rising along my backbone, and a cold chill passed through my entire body. I took a step backward. "Drover, listen carefully. We're fixing to go into Red Alert."

"Didn't I tell you they weren't buzzards?"

"No. Yes. I don't know what you said, and it doesn't matter. What matters is that those things don't belong to this world."

"Yeah, I tried to tell you."

"Will you please hush? On the count of three, we will go into our Red Alert Drill, only this isn't a drill. Ready? Three!"

ZOOM. Fellers, I ran.

Behind me, I heard Drover's voice. "Wait, what about one and two?"

"I'm trying to trick them! To the bunkers!"

Well, I told you this was going to turn into a scary story, and maybe you didn't believe me. Now you know the awful truth, and the awful truth is pretty awful.

I went streaking down the hill to the gas tanks and dived under my gunnysack bed. Moments later, I heard Drover's huffing and puffing, and he dived under his bed. An eerie silence spread across the whole world, and I reached for the microphone of my mind.

"Peaches, this is Rhubarb. Switch to Emergency Frequency. Do you copy?"

"You told me to run on the count of three, but you didn't say one and two."

"Drover, when we go up against dinosaur birds, we must use stealth and cunning. They're extremely dangerous."

"I told you they were dinosaur birds, but you didn't believe me. I was right, wasn't I?"

I pondered his question. "Drover, if I admit that you were right, you must promise never to tell anyone."

"How come?"

"Because . . . because it really hurts to admit that you're right. I won't do it unless you promise not to tell."

"Well, okay. I promise."

I took a big gulp of air, squared my shoulders, and prepared to deliver a brutal confession. "All right, Drover, I'm about to speak three words that I have rarely used in my career, and they're going to hurt me more than you can imagine. You. Were. Right."

We Send Out a Scout Patrol

Suddenly I heard a burst of strange noises coming from outside my bunker. "Tee hee hee hee hee!"

"Drover, I just heard an explosion of peculiar sounds. It wasn't you, was it?"

"No, it wasn't tee hee."

"Oh, good. There for a second I thought you were laughing and gloating."

"Oh, heck no, not me hee. It must have been those dinosaur birds."

"Hmmm. Good point. It stands to reason that they would make some kind of chirping sound."

"Yeah. What I heard was, 'Tee hee hee hee hee hee hee!'"

"Exactly. Tell you what; let's exit the bunkers. I'll meet you outside in three seconds. Go!"

Three seconds later, we met in daily broadlight outside our bunkers. In the broadlight of day, I noticed that Drover was grinning. "Why are you wearing that silly grin?"

"Who, me hee? I didn't know I was grinning."

"You were and still are. Wipe that smirk off your mouth, soldier. We have important business to discuss."

Drover wiped the silly grin off his mouth, and we got down to some serious business. First thing, I did a complete Three-Sixty Scan of the surrounding territory. In a Three-Sixty, we swing our gaze around in a complete circle, just to be sure we're not being spied upon by cats or enemy spies or even chickens. In this line of work, we never know where danger might be lurking.

Take those chickens, for example. They run loose during the day and spend a lot of time loitering around headquarters, pecking gravel and various insects. Sometimes their loitering brings them close to our Secured Areas, and naturally that makes us suspicious. We're never sure if they're just being dumb chickens or if they're actually enemy agents wearing chicken suits, so we watch 'em closely.

So I did my Three-Sixty Scan and . . . Did I mention that our Scanning Devices don't turn the full three hundred and sixty degrees? They don't. They'll turn about half the circle and at that point they lock down. Sometimes during this lockdown event, a dog will lose his balance and, well, topple over backward.

That's what happened, but here's the strange part. Apparently the dinosaur birds were spying on us, because when I hit the ground with a thud, I heard the same chattering sounds we had heard before: "Tee hee, tee hee, tee hee!"

I picked myself off the ground and rolled a couple of kinks out of my back. "Drover, I think those birds are *laughing* at us."

His gaze drifted up to the clouds. "I'll be derned. I never would have hee hee thought of that."

"What?"

"I said, I never would have thought of that."

"Yes, and that's why I'm here, son. The analysis of intelligence intercepts requires intelligence and . . . well, you come up a little short in that department."

"Yeah, but I've always tried to be tall."

"Good for you. Never give up hope." I narrowed my eyes and gazed off into the pasture. The birds were still there. "Okay, this has gone far enough.

We can't just sit here and allow those birds to make a mockery of the entire Security Division."

"Yeah, what a couple of rats."

"Here's the plan. We're going to send out a scout patrol. We must find out what they're doing on our ranch."

"Great idea!"

"And Drover"—I laid a paw on his shoulder—"we're looking for volunteers."

His eyes blanked out. "Volunteers for what?"

"We need one good man to lead the scout patrol."

"Yeah, but I'm just a dog."

"That's what I mean. We need one good dog, and this could lead to a big promotion . . . if you should happen to come back alive, of course."

"You said I was too short."

"Height is not an issue here."

"Yeah, but . . ." He shrank back and placed a paw over his chest. "You remember that heart problem we were talking about? Boy, this old heart is really starting to flutter."

"That's what hearts do."

"Yeah, but not like this." Suddenly he began wheezing and coughing, his eyes crossed, and he tumbled over backward on the ground. "Oh drat,

there it went! First the leg and now the heart! Oh my heart, oh my leg!"

I beamed a steely gaze at the little mutter-mumble. I knew he was faking this, I KNEW it, but...well, the heart problem was something new, and I sure didn't want to run the risk that, for the first time in his whole life, he might be telling the truth. Weird things like that can happen, you know.

So what's a guy to do?

"All right, I'll lead the mission. I'll win the medals for bravery, and you'll spend the rest of your life brooding over all the opportunities you missed."

"I know; I hate it. The guilt's already starting to eat at me."

"Good. I'm leaving you in charge of the relief column."

"Boy, that's a relief."

"If I'm not back in half an hour, send fresh troops. We have no idea what we'll be facing out there, but we could get ourselves into some serious combat." I whirled around, pointed myself toward the north, and began marching off to...I knew not what.

Was I scared? Of course I was scared. Nobody in our Security Division had ever gone up against a pair of dinosaur birds. We'd had no training in Terradogtail Defense. Our combat manuals had nothing about their weapons or tactics, such as... what did they do with those oversized beaks? Did they have teeth...poison stingers...laser weapons that could reduce a dog to a puff of smoke?

You bet I was scared, but the job had to be done and my assistant was just too much of a chicken to do it.

I had gone, oh, maybe twenty steps when I heard an odd sound. "Tee hee hee."

I stopped, froze, lifted one ear, and listened. The sound had stopped. I whirled around. "Drover, did you say something?"

"Me? Well, let me think. No, it wasn't me hee."

"I'm almost sure I heard someone say, 'Tee hee hee.'"

"Oh, that. Yeah, it was those birds again. I guess they're really laughing it up."

I squared my enormous shoulders. "Well, let 'em laugh while they can. At the end of the day, we'll see who's laughing."

"Yeah, and it won't be them hee hee."

"Thanks, Drover. You're a little weenie sometimes, but at least your heart's in the right place."

"Yeah, it's feeling a little better now."

"Really? Then why don't you . . ." He collapsed and began kicking his legs in the air. "Never mind. I'll be better off without you."

"Oh, the guilt!"

With Drover's moans echoing in my ears, I marched away from headquarters and set my sights on the two large, mysterious dinosaur birds that were lurking in my pasture.

I had come up with a plan of battle, and it was pretty simple: no battle. No sir, before I jumped into combat with a couple of dinosaur birds, I needed to do a little spying and gather some information.

Creeping from bush to bush and weed to weed, I inched forward until I was able to establish a Forward Listening Post, maybe twenty yards away from the birds. Actually, I was kind of surprised that I was able to get so close without being detected.

Don't forget, they had Bacon Radar. Hmmm. Maybe Bacon Radar only worked on bacon, and . . . well, I wasn't bacon. That made sense.

They appeared to be in the midst of an argument, so absorbed in their own conversation, they didn't notice me. That was good. I wasn't quite ready to announce myself.

Anyway, let's run through a description of these rare dinosaur birds. They were as big as geese and had long skinny legs with webbed feet fastened to the ends of their legs; brown feathers all around except on the underside, which was white; broad wingspread, about as wide as a buzzard's; and a head...

That was the part I couldn't believe. It was about the weirdest head I'd ever seen or even thought about seeing. It was mostly BEAK except for a pair of little eyes, and we're talking about a beak that was two feet long!

These were very strange-looking creatures. No wonder they had almost vanished from the face of the Earth. They looked so silly, they had been invited to leave.

Crouching flat against the ground, I activated Earatory Scanners and began pulling in their conversation. Right away, I was able to establish their names and identities. The bigger and younger of the two was named Freddy. The other of the two appeared to be a little old woman, and Freddy called her Momma. This led me to suspect that maybe Freddy was the son and Momma was... well, his mother, and maybe that's obvious.

Anyway, they were involved in some kind of heavy discussion, and Momma seemed to be in a bad mood. Here, let's switch on the speakers so you can listen.

I Meet a Real Dinosaur Bird

Are you ready to listen in on a conversation between two Terradogtail Dinosaur Birds? Here we go.

[Speakers on. Quiet! Roll tape.]

Momma: You never look at a map.
Freddy: Now, Momma . . .
Momma: You never ask for directions.
Freddy: Now, Momma . . .
Momma: You never stop for food. You just fly, fly, fly, and now we're as lost as a couple of bunny rabbits!
Freddy: Momma, we're not lost. I think we're in Port Isabel. See, there's the lighthouse right over yonder.

Momma: That ain't a lighthouse, it's a windmill!

Freddy: Now, Momma, sometimes you're right, but this time you're wrong. We don't have windmills on the Gulf Coast.

Momma covered her face with both wings and let out a moan. "Freddy, that's what I've been trying to tell you for the past three days. This ain't the Gulf Coast! You flew right into the middle of a hurricane and have got us so lost, we'll never get back."

Freddy squinted at a windmill in the distance. "You know, it does look a little bit like a windmill, don't it?"

"Because it is a windmill!"

"Shhh. Momma, don't talk so loud. Somebody might be listening."

"Let 'em listen, I don't give a rip. Take me home!"

Freddy glanced around in a full circle. "Uh . . . Momma, we need to talk. Remember that left turn we made at Harlingen? I'm thinking maybe we should have gone straight."

Momma stared at him with an open beak. "Straight? That's what I told you!"

"Momma, sometimes you mumble your words."

"Well, I ain't mumbling now. You have brung me out into the desert!"

Freddy seemed at a loss for words. He shuffled his feet and glanced around. "Well, it's kind of a pretty desert. Look at all the nice cactus."

"I don't want to look at the cactus! Take me home!"

At that very moment, Freddy's gaze landed on me. His eyes popped wide-open, and he let out a gasp. "Momma, be real quiet. I think I'm seeing a wolf over yonder in some weeds."

"A wolf!"

"Shh, not so loud. Yes, it's a wolf. See? Lookie yonder."

Freddy pointed a wing at me. Momma squinted her eyes. "That's a dog, Freddy."

"No, ma'am, that's a wolf."

"He don't look smart enough to be a wolf."

Freddy took a closer look. "You could be right. Maybe he's a dog, sure 'nuff."

"He's a dog. Go ask him where we're at."

"Momma, what if he tries to eat me?"

"Don't let him."

"Well . . ." Freddy nodded his head and shuffled his feet. "I guess I could try. You wait right here. I don't imagine this'll take long."

"Ask him which way's the ocean."

"Momma, I can handle this. You just try to be calm, hear?"

Freddy clasped his wings behind his back and began shuffling in my direction. It appeared that I was about to get acquainted with a genuine Terradogtail Dinosaur Bird.

He came waddling up to me, and when I say "waddling," I mean *waddling*. The guy walked like a duck, swinging his body back and forth, and his face . . . that was the oddest face I'd ever seen, all beak and two little eyes. Under different circumstances, I might have laughed out loud, but this was the wrong time to be laughing.

Never estimunderate your enemy, I always say. The ones who look the silliest might turn out to be the most dangerous. Silliness can be a clever disguise.

He walked up to me and stopped. "Hi there. We seen you in the weeds. How are the weeds today?"

Well, I had been exposed, and there was no need in trying to pretend that I wasn't there, so I rose to my full height and gave him a stern glare. "The weeds are swell."

"Good, good. Say, you ain't a wolf, are you?"

"I'm a dog."

"Oh good. That's what Momma said, but I wasn't sure."

"Hank the Cowdog, Head of Ranch Security. I'm here to conduct an interrogation. What are you doing here?"

He scowled. "Well, Momma and I were just talking about that, and the truth is...we might be lost." He glanced around. "Which way's the beach?"

"We don't have a beach."

"How far is it to Port Isabel?"

"Never heard of it."

"Well, that's not good." He turned to his mother. "Momma, he says he's never heard of Port Isabel."

She threw her wings in the air. "See? I knew it!"

He turned back to me. "Well sir, I guess we're lost, sure 'nuff." He grinned and stuck out his right wing. "Name's Freddy."

I paced away from him. "We know your name, Freddy, and this isn't a social occasion. We've had you under surveillance for weeks. We know that you made a wrong turn, flew into a hurricane, got blown off course, and landed here—illegally, I might add. You thought that windmill over there was a lighthouse, and your mother's mad at you." I whirled around and faced him. "How am I doing?"

He was amazed. "I'll be switched. How'd you know all that?"

"Surveillance, Freddy. It's what we do. We've put together a huge file. We know that you stole the bacon—don't bother to deny it; we have a witness. We even know how you did it, with a secret weapon called a Bacon Beacon."

"No sir, we thought it was a lighthouse, but it turned out to be a windmill. See it over yonder?" He pointed his wing to the north. "Windmills don't have a beacon."

The air hissed out of my lungs, and I paced away from him. This was going nowhere. Was Freddy as dumb as he seemed, or was this some kind of clever anti-interrogation technique? At this point, I didn't know.

"Okay, Freddy, let's try another question. Do you eat dogs? I must know."

He rocked up and down on his toes and scowled. "Well, I don't, but let me ask Momma." He yelled, "Momma, he wants to know if you've ever ate a dog!"

She screeched, "Ate a dog! What are y'all doing over there?"

"Well, he's a guard dog and he's asking questions and... I don't know. He wants to know if you've ever ate a dog."

"No! I eat fish! Quit fooling around and take me home!"

Freddy turned back to me and shrugged. "She eats fish."

I heaved a sigh of relief. "That's good news."

"Well, it ain't so good if you're in the middle of a desert. Momma gets a little cranky when she don't get her morning fish."

"Freddy, it's good news that dinosaur birds don't eat dogs. If she did, you and I would be drawn into a deadly... Why are you staring at me?"

His beak had dropped open, and his eyes were wide. "Did you say that my momma looks like a *dinosaur*?"

"Well... yes, of course I did. Look at her, Freddy. Is that a hummingbird? A warbler?" Suddenly it dawned on me that I had blundered into a family secret. "You haven't told her? She doesn't know her true identity?"

Freddy's silence said it all. The poor woman was a living fossil, and her own son hadn't told her!

Well, I hadn't planned on spending half my day doing family counseling with a couple of prehistoric relics, but... well, there was something about this case that touched my heart. I mean,

Freddy struck me as kind of a goofball but, on the whole, a decent sort of fellow.

It was obvious that this family was in a crisis. Would I help them or just send them down the road?

I Try to Help a Family in Need

In my line of work, we have to guard against being tenderhearted. That's why we wrap ourselves in layer after layer of steel and iron. That's why the general public thinks that we Heads of Ranch Security have no feelings. We're tough because we have to be tough, but once in a while...

I began pacing back and forth, as I often do when my mind is trying to wrap itself around the taco meat of Life. "We know all about your secret. Your mother's a dinosaur, and you've never told her. Fredly, Frankie, I'm shocked that you've withheld the truth. What kind of son are you, anyway?"

He thought about that for a minute. "Well, I'm the kind that don't have nerve enough to tell his momma she's a dinosaur."

"That's exactly my point, Frankie. She needs to know." I stopped pacing and delivered my next words in a firm voice. *"She looks totally weird and doesn't even know why!"*

His eyes bugged out. "You think my momma looks weird?"

"Of course I do! Look at her! Look at that nose!"

He squinted at his mother. "Well . . . she looks just like me, only a hundred years old."

"Frank, she looks like... may I call you Frank? I mean, *Frankie* sounds a little childish, don't you think? At some point, we have to grow up." I resumed my pacing. "Frank, your mother looks like a Terradogtail Dinosaur... *because she is,* and she deserves to know why everyone laughs when she walks down the street!"

He took a step backward. "Who's been laughing at my momma?"

"Frank, listen to me. I'm speaking to you as a friend. Our mothers give us their love and devotion. The least we can do is tell them the truth."

He scratched the top of his head with the tip of his wing. "Well, I have to admit there's been times when I thought she looked a little old-fashioned."

"There we go! You've made the first step toward the truth. Fossils always look old-fashioned. It's a reality that can't be denied. Just tell her."

He rolled his eyes up to the sky. "She ain't going to like this."

"It might hurt her feelings at first, but in the long run, she'll be glad to know. I mean, deep inside, we all crave the truth. We want to know who we are and where we came from."

"Well, that don't sound exactly like Momma, but if you think we ought to tell her..."

"I do, Frank, I really do." I placed a paw across his back. "Come on, pal; I'll go with you and give you some moral support. Everyone will feel a lot better when this is out in the open. Let's go."

Together, my new friend and I walked toward the poor lady with the outrageous beak. It was a pretty touching moment. Just think about it. These birds and I were separated by thousands of years. They were living fossils, and I belonged to the modern age. We were different in every way you can imagine, yet our lives had been brought together by a simple yearning for The Truth.

It almost brought tears to my eyes. There I was, a very important dog, befriending the homeliest birds I had ever seen. Did I laugh at them, call them names, make fun of their appearance? No sir. The fact that they were incredibly ugly hardly even entered my mind.

Okay, it entered my mind. Who could ignore it?

But the important thing is that I didn't dwell upon the differences between us. I looked instead to the qualities beneath the skin and hair and feathers, the qualities that pointed to the Brotherhood of All Animals.

And fellers, you talk about an emotional scene! Words could hardly express how wonderful I felt about myself as I marched side by side with the second-ugliest bird in the whole world. (His mother was in first place.)

We walked up to her and stopped. Her head jerked around and, yipes, she already looked crabby, and we hadn't even given her any bad news. Frank reached out a wing and gave her a pat. "Momma, this here is . . . what was your name again?"

"Hank the Cowdog."

"That's right. You're Hank and I'm Freddy."

"I thought you were Frank."

"No, I'm Freddy, been Freddy all my life. Freddy Pelican."

"Pelican? Is that French?"

"Thousand Island." He gave me a wink and chuckled to himself. Was that funny? He thought so, but I had no time for jokes. His grin faded, and he turned back to his mother. "Momma, this here is Hank the Cowdog. He's in charge of security around here."

Her gaze stuck me like a fork. "What does he think, we're going to rob a bank?"

"Momma, just listen. Hank's an important feller, and there's something he wants to tell you." He turned to me and gave me an expectant nod. "Go ahead, Hank."

"I thought you were going to tell her."

"Well, no, I figured . . . Momma, excuse us for just a second." Freddy and I went off to the side to discuss our business. He whispered, "I figured you'd want to tell her."

"Hey, Freddy, she's your mother. She might not appreciate hearing bad news from a stranger. She needs to hear this from her own son."

Freddy rocked up and down on his toes, deep in thought. "You reckon? The thing is, I'd hate to mess it up, you know, say the wrong thing."

"You'll do fine. Just tell her the truth. When you stick with the truth, what can go wrong?"

He thought about that. "Well, quite a lot, I 'spect, but if you're sure . . ."

"I'm sure, Freddy. This is a time for a son to share the truth with his mother."

"Ooooo-kay. Let's do it."

We walked back to her. I could almost feel the

tension in the air, the kind of tension that comes before a moment of Healing Truth.

Freddy took a deep breath and said, "Momma, Hank wanted me to tell you that *you look like an old dinosaur*."

Huh?

I stared at Freddy, unable to believe that he'd said what he'd said. I mean, he had more or less spoken the truth, but for crying out loud...

Boys, you talk about a DEAD SILENCE. We had one. You could have heard a pin feather drop.

Momma's eyes widened and she asked, "What did you say?"

I held a paw to my lips, hoping that Freddy would get the message to hush. He didn't hush. He raised his voice and said, *"This dog says you look like an old dinosaur!"*

I caught Freddy by the wing and led him off to the side. "What are you trying to do, get me murdered?"

"Well, I just told her what you said."

"That's not what I said. I said she IS a dinosaur, not that she looks like one. A lady might *be* a dinosaur, but no lady wants to *look* like one."

He heaved a sigh. "That's why I wanted you to do the talking. I've never had a way with words."

"Yes, well, foolish me. I should have listened. Okay, I'd better handle it from here."

"Oh, good, 'cause I've got a feeling Momma's fixing to be on the peck."

Peck? I glanced at her long beak. It was sharp on the end. Clearly, I would have to choose my words with care.

We turned back to Momma and I faced her with a big, warm . . . yipes. She had folded her wings across her chest, and her head seemed to have sunk into her shoulders. And there was a storm in her eyes.

I addressed her in a soothing tone of voice. "Uh, ma'am, we've had a little misunderstanding here. See, I was misquoted, and maybe you'd like to, uh, hear a clarification of my remarks. What do you say?" She said nothing, just stabbed me with a cold gaze. "Anyway, what I told Freddy was an obvious fact: you're a Terradogtail Dinosaur Bird. I wasn't making any judgments. I just think you're entitled to know about your, uh, cultural heritage . . . don't you see."

Her hawkish gaze flicked over to Freddy. "What's he talking about?"

Freddy looked very uncomfortable. "Momma, you remind him of a dinosaur, some kind of freak."

Her eyes snapped back to me. "Freak!"

I searched my mind for a tactful way of putting this. “Now, ma’am, I didn’t say that. Let’s just say that a dinosaur living in the present day is . . . well, unique. Distinctive.”

Momma’s eyes came at me like bullets. “Freak, huh? Old dinosaur?” Her head rose out of her shoulders. Her eyes were on fire. She began loosening up her wings, almost as though . . .

I began backing away. “Now, ma’am, there’s no need to . . . What we have here is a failure to communicate. Freddy, do something with your mother!”

“Ha. You’re on your own.”

“Coward! Listen, ma’am, I think I can explain everything. My only point was . . .”

BAM! BLAP!

Drover Gets Thrown in Jail

You know, she'd looked old and shriveled and decrepit, but when she flew into the middle of me, I thought I'd walked into an airplane propeller. I mean, you talk about getting thrashed by a pair of wings!

And remember that long, ridiculous beak? When she turned it into a jackhammer and started using it on the top of my head, nobody was laughing. I sure wasn't.

Well, I thought I'd never get away from the old bat, but at last I broke away and staggered out of her range. Freddy came hopping after me, wearing a look of deep concern.

"Are you all right? Brother, you've got some knots on your head! Did Momma do all that?"

I rubbed my throbbing head. "What do you think? Those aren't mosquito bites."

"Yes, she gets riled up sometimes. I had a feeling she would. Momma's awful sensitive about her age."

"Yeah? Well, thanks for warning me."

"You know, I tried but . . ." He gave me a wink. ". . . you don't listen too good."

I stuck my nose in his face. "You know, pal, I liked you at first and even felt sorry for you because you look like a fossil and your mother's a lunatic; but after getting better acquainted, I've changed my mind. Get off my ranch and don't come back!"

He was shocked. "Well, you don't need to get all hateful. Me and Momma never wanted to be a burden."

"You're a burden. Thanks to you and your big mouth, I've got thirty-seven knots on my head."

He swallowed a lump in his throat, and mist came to his eyes. "Well, Momma's been in poor health, and I . . . I just don't know where to go."

"Poor health! She almost chopped my head off!" I stuck my nose in his face and gave him a snarl. "Look, I'm not running a rest home for dinosaurs."

His face grew solemn. "You keep talking about dinosaurs."

"Because that's what you are—a couple of

living, breathing, squawking, bacon-stealing fossils. I'm sorry you're lost, and I hope you find your way back to wherever you belong, but get off my ranch. You've got five minutes to clear out."

Freddy gave his head a sad shake and waddled back to his mother. "Momma, he says we have to leave. We're not welcome here."

"The hateful old thing!" She covered her face with both wings and began to cry. "Oh, Freddy, I just want to go home!"

He gave her a hug. "I know, Momma, and we'll try our best." He turned to me and waved his wing. "Well, thanks for all your kindness. We'll probably . . . we'll probably be all right."

And with that, they flapped their big wings and flew out of my life.

I know what you're thinking—that I was a rat for throwing them off my ranch. Isn't that what you were thinking? Be honest.

Well, I don't care. The Head of Ranch Security has to make tough decisions and sometimes . . . Hey, look at the facts. They were a couple of ugly fossil birds who would never fit into life on a modern ranch. They needed to go back to Dinosaur Land and enjoy life amongst the other fossils.

And don't forget that they'd stolen my breakfast bacon, right from under my very nose. I mean, that's a serious crime, and I could have thrown the book at them. If you ask me, they got off pretty lucky.

So if you want to waste your time worrying about Freddy and his weird momma, go right ahead, but I had more important things to do—a ranch to run, patrols to make, reports to write. I was a very busy dog, and busy dogs don't have time to brood about homeless birds.

I made my way back to the office. Drover was there, but I didn't speak to him. This Dinosaur Case had worn me out and I needed a nap, so I flopped down on my gunnysack bed.

Drover was watching. "How'd it go?"

"It went great. I ordered them off the ranch and warned them never to come back. No problem. Good night." I closed my eyes and tried to drift off to sleep.

"How'd you get all those knots on your head?"

I sat up and beamed him a glare of steel. "If you must know, Mister Snoop, the old lady drilled me with her beak."

"I'll be derned. I wonder why she did that."

"Who knows? She's unstable. And I guess she didn't appreciate being reminded that she's a dinosaur." I noticed that he was grinning. "Did I say something funny?"

"Well, yeah, sort of. I don't think she's a dinosaur."

"Of course she's a dinosaur. Little Alfred said so. The boy knows everything about dinosaurs."

"Yeah, but after you left, Sally May got out the bird book, and she found a match."

"She burned the book?"

"No, she found a picture that *matched* those birds." A grin spread across his mouth. "They're pelicans."

All at once, half-forgotten clues began flooding my mind. "Wait a second, hold everything. Those birds were lost, looking for a lighthouse, and Freddy even called himself 'Freddy Pelican'! I thought it was just an odd French name, but it was actually . . . Don't you get it, Drover? *They're pelicans!*"

"Yeah, that's what I said."

I had to indulge myself in a little chuckle. "Well, no wonder the old bat got so mad when I called her a dinosaur. Ha ha." Suddenly I had a great idea. "Drover, those birds are so ridiculous, we should sing a song about them."

He thought about that. "Yeah, it might be fun...only we don't know any songs about pelicans."

"We'll make it up as we go along. You do a verse, I'll do a verse, and we'll see where it goes." And with that, we belted out a great little song called "Why Does a Pelican Look So Bizarre?" You'll love this.

Why Does a Pelican Look So Bizarre?

I wonder who built the first pelican, this
highly unusual bird.
The way he's put together brings to mind the
term "absurd."
He sounds like a seagull and looks like a dork.
He stands on two legs that resemble a stork.
They're stuck on a body the shape of a cork.

Why does a pelican look so bizarre?

I wonder who drew up the blueprint that
yielded the basic design
Of a dinosaur pterodactyl who got lost in the
tunnel of time?
What does he eat? A fish now and then.
He carries a basket right under his chin.
His beak is so long he can't muster a grin.
Why does a pelican look so bizarre?

What thoughts do you reckon his mother had
when she looked into his bed.
Imagine the shock of seeing that thing! You
wonder what she said.
Maybe she fainted and fell on the floor.
Maybe she screamed and ran out the door.
Or maybe she issued a laugh like a roar:
"Why does my baby look so bizarre?"

A mother will love most any old thing that
falls into her care.
She'll feed it and hold it and rock it to sleep
and dress it in underwear.
But pelican mothers are put to the test.
You can hardly imagine the level of stress
With something so ugly right there in her
nest.

Why does a pelican look so bizarre?

We're all part of God's creation; He made us in different styles.
The day He constructed a pelican, He must have been wearing a smile.
For here was a joke in a feathery suit,
Wearing that highly ridiculous snoot,
As long as your arm but with nary a tooth.
A pelican looks like a cosmic gaffe,
So maybe he's here to give us a laugh.

Pretty amazing song, huh? You bet, and don't forget that we made it up on the spot. We laughed and celebrated our masterpiece, then Drover said, "But you know what? It gets even funnier, 'cause they didn't steal your bacon."

I stared at him. "What?"

"Hee hee. It was Pete."

For a moment I couldn't speak. "Pete! That's impossible. I was standing right there."

"Yeah, and so was I. While you were looking up at the pelicans, I saw the whole thing. Pete dashed over, snatched up your pieces of bacon, and gobbled 'em down."

"Nonsense. You'll never convince me..."

A deadly silence moved over us. In the back of my mind, I reconstructed the scene at Scrap Time:

me on the left, Drover in the middle, and Pete over on the right. Yet when I discovered that my bacon was gone, Drover was on the right, I stood in the middle, and Pete had moved over...to the *left side*!

Pete had sneaked past me and I hadn't noticed.

He hadn't taken even one bite out of his biscuit, remember?!

And when he burped, I SMELLED BACON!

My whole body went limp and I collapsed on the ground. For several long moments, I lay there on my back, twitching and blinking my eyes, while the rest of the world spun around in dizzy circles. At last I was able to sit up.

"He did it, he really did it, and all that stuff about the Beacon Bacon was just a cruel hoax." I took a big gulp of fresh air and tried to steady my nerves. "Drover, you know what hurts most about this disgraceful affair?"

"Well, let's see. You insulted a nice old lady?"

"No, worse than that."

"All those knots on your head?"

"Even worse than the knots."

He frowned and rolled his eyes around. "Well, let's see. You got skunked by the cat?"

"No." I pushed myself up on wobbly legs, stuck my nose in his face, and screamed, "Traitor! You saw the whole thing and didn't tell me!"

"Well, I tried, but you wouldn't listen."

"Our Security Division has suffered a crushing humiliation and *it was all your fault*!" My screams echoed into the distance, and I sank to the ground. "Drover, we're ruined, and the worst part, the very darkest and ugliest part, is that . . . it *wasn't* your fault."

He stared at me with an open mouth. "I thought you just said . . ."

"Drover, I did it to myself. I fell for every one of Pete's tricks. Sometimes I think I'm not very smart."

A silly grin wiggled across his mouth. "Boy, I'm glad to hear you say that."

"Glad? It rips my heart out!"

"Yeah, but I've never had the nerve to tell you."

There was a long moment of silence. My eyes locked on him. Suddenly I felt a rush of fresh energy coursing through my body. I rose to my full height and towered over the slandering little wretch. "Did you just say that your commanding officer isn't as smart as he thinks he is?"

His grin faded. "Well, that's what you said."

"Soldier, you're going to the brig. Move!"

Hanging his head in shame, the little traitor shuffled over to the northwest angle iron leg of the gas tank platform and stuck his nose in the corner. "I was just trying to be honest."

"Then let this be a lesson to you. There's a time to be honest, and there's a time to keep your trap shut."

"How long do I have to stay in jail?"

"Weeks. Months. You may never see the light of day again."

"Oh, rats." After a moment of silence, he said, "Wait! I think I've got the answer!"

We Find the Answer to Life

I had begun scratching a flea on my right ear. When I heard Drover's words, my leg froze in midair. "The answer? The answer to what?"

"Our problem. Everything. Life."

"You have the Answer to Life?"

"Yeah, you want to hear it?"

I hoisted myself up to a standing position and paced over to his cell. "Is this some kind of joke?"

"Nope, I just thought of it." He gave me a mysterious look and whispered, "Let's go chase the cat!"

My first response was to laugh out loud. "Ha ha. Chase the cat? That's the Answer to Life?" But then . . . hmmm . . . I found myself pacing back and forth in front of Drover's dingy cell. "You know, that's not as crazy as you might think. In fact . . . Drover, it was the cat that started this whole mess. Think about it. He made a monkey out of me, and I made a jailbird out of you. He's turned us against each other, dog against dog!"

I stopped in my tracks and whirled around. "Don't you get it? This could be the Answer to Life Itself! Any time we're sad, any time we're feeling depressed, we can always chase the cat and run him up a tree! Drover, this could be a cure for everything. Why didn't I think of this sooner?"

"I don't know, but can I get out of jail?"

I gave that some thought. "Have you learned a lesson from this?"

"Oh yeah. I can't remember it right now, but it was a great lesson."

"That's close enough." I inserted the key into the cell door and threw it open. "Drover, you are now a free dog. Let's go chase the cat!"

The little mutt rushed out into the sunlight and began doing rolls on the ground. "Oh, freedom!"

"Come on, son, to the yard!"

We launched ourselves into the morning breeze and flew in tight formation all the way down to the house. Ten yards out, we executed a perfect landing and coasted to a stop. I climbed out of the cockpit and turned to Drover.

"All right, men, are we ready to chase a cat?"

Drover was jumping around and throwing punches in the air. "You bet, just let me at 'im!"

"That's the spirit. Form a line and follow me, we're going in!"

I had already drawn up a plan for this mission. Would you like to see it? I guess it wouldn't hurt to release it to the general public.

The plan was pretty simple and straightforward. Since the enemy spent most of his pampered life inside the yard, we would have to breach the walls of the city. It would be difficult but not impossible. Our troops would have to leap upward, hook our front paws on the rim of the fortress walls, pull ourselves up and over, then sprint across the open courtyard to the iris patch.

Once we had the area secured, we would move in and . . . heh heh . . . chase the little snot all the way into next week. The Security Division would be restored to its previous greatness, and we would experience the sheer joy of . . .

Huh?

What I saw in the distance caused me to stop in my tracks. "Company, halt!"

Drover wasn't paying attention (he never does) and ran into me. "Oops, sorry. What's the deal?"

"We have to cancel the mission. Look." I pointed

BOINK

a paw toward the house. Pete sat on the porch—smirking at us, purring, and rubbing on Sally May, who was also sitting on the porch . . . peeling carrots.

Oh, and get this. When he saw us, Kitty sat up straight and waved a paw.

Drover and I turned our backs on the cat and went into a huddle. Drover was the first to speak. "Gosh, what'll we do now?"

"We can't risk sending troops over the wall. With Sally May sitting there, it would be suicide."

"Oops. We don't need that."

"Exactly. She's armed with a carrot peeler, and her broom can't be far away." My mind was racing. "Okay, here's the backup plan." Before I could reveal the plan, Drover began backing away. "What are you doing?"

"I thought you said to back up."

"No, I said . . ."

ZOOM. It happened so fast, I saw only a small cloud of dust and a white comet streaking toward the machine shed. Then I heard a faint voice in the distance. "Boy, this old leg's really starting to throb, oh, my leg!" And he was gone.

Oh well, I wouldn't need his help anyway, because the next phase of the mission called for a delicate diplomatic effort. See, under a flag of truce, I would try to lure the cat out of the yard, away from Sally May, and then . . . well, you can guess.

As I always say, when brute force fails, try charm. If charm works, you can always go back to brute force. Heh heh.

I walked toward the yard gate holding up my flag of truce. "Pete? We need to talk."

His eyes sparkled. "Oh, really? What fun!" He scampered off the porch and came bounding down the sidewalk. "I just love talking to you, Hankie. What now?"

There he was, sitting only two feet away from me with nothing but a wire fence between us. Before I could think, my ears leaped up and my lips began rippling into a snarl. I had to shut everything down before my savage instincts gave me away.

I beamed him a pleasant smile. "Hi, Pete, great to see you again, no kidding."

"Oh, really? Somehow I find that hard to believe, Hankie." He leaned toward me and whispered, "How were the dinosaurs? Hee hee."

Boy, you talk about Iron Discipline. Every cell in my enormous body was calling for me to hamburgerize the little creep, but somehow I managed to stay in control. "Say, Pete, that was a great prank. Pelicans, and I fell for it. Ha ha. I mean, I really thought they were dinosaur birds."

"I know you did. I couldn't believe it." He let out a snicker and whispered behind his paw, "Did you figure out what happened to your bacon?"

I froze. Could I go on with this? Yes, I had to. "Ha ha. I did, Pete, and I've got to hand it to you, pal, that may have been the best joke you've ever pulled."

He sputtered with laughter. "Right under your nose!"

Speaking of my nose, at that very moment it was trying to point itself at the cat like the barrel of a gun. With great effort, I moved it away from the, uh, target. "Boy, what a silly goose I was! Ha ha. Great prank, Pete, you win first prize. And you know what, Pete?" I turned an innocent gaze toward the clouds above. "I deserved it. I had it coming."

He stared at me with hooded eyes. "Oh, really?"

"No kidding, I'm being sincere. In fact . . . hey, Pete, here's an idea. Why don't we go for a walk and, you know, talk and laugh about old times, huh? Just the two of us. What do you think?"

The end of his tail began to twitch. "You're not bitter?"

"Bitter? Me?" I almost choked, trying to keep a

growl from roaring up my throat. “Not at all. No, I think it’s important that we, uh, see the humor in our various life experiences and . . . well, share them together.”

Oops. My lips were twitching again. This was tough, but my plan seemed to be working.

Kitty stared at me with his weird yellow eyes. “You know, Hankie, I’m amazed. You seem to have undergone a complete transformation.”

“Right, and you know, Pete, it was time for a change. I mean, a guy can’t spend his whole life being angry and bitter, know what I mean? I lost, you won, it’s history, and, hey, let’s go for a little stroll and share a few laughs. What do you say?”

“Well, Hankie, this seems to be the dawning of a new day.”

“Right, exactly, and that’s a great way of putting it.”

“But Hankie, I have one concern. May I confide in you?”

“Oh, sure, you bet. Hey, that’s what friends are for.”

He motioned for me to move closer to the fence, so that my ear was only inches away from his cheating little . . . uh, from his mouth, let us say. And he whispered, “Hankie, I smell a rat.”

“A rat? You mean, like a rodent rat?”

"No, no. It's more of a canine rat."

"A canine rat? That's odd. 'Canine' means 'dog,' right?"

"Um-hm. Watch this."

Before my very eyes, he took a big gulp of air, humped his back, opened his mouth wide, and HISSED in my face! And what was I supposed to do, sit there and be Mister Doggie Wonderful? No way. I had been bushwhacked, so naturally I . . . well, I barked. And we're talking about deep, manly barks.

Oops.

I watched in complete amazement as the treacherous little hickocrip began limping in circles, dragging one leg and moaning in a pitiful voice. "He bit me, I'm wounded! Sally May, help me!"

Uh-oh. Sally May launched herself off the porch like a rocket, scattering carrot peelings in all directions. "Hank, leave the cat alone, you big bully!"

Huh? Me?

I beamed her Looks of Sainthood and went to Slow Wags on the tail section.

Leave the cat alone? I hadn't laid a paw on the little snake! This was all show business, a shabby little circus that was intended to get me in deep . . . oh, brother, here she came, storming in my direction.

For one brief moment, I considered standing my ground and arguing my case in the Court of Sally May, using all of my many gifts of persuasion: Sincere Wags, Sad Ears, and Looks of Remorse. But something about her manner convinced me that things had gotten out of hand. Maybe it was the steam hissing out of her ears.

Anyway, it came to me in a flash that the only honorable solution to this crisis was to . . . well, run.

I sold the farm and ran, but managed to fire off one last shot over my shoulder. "Pete, you'll pay for this!"

Exactly how or when he would pay wasn't clear at that desperate moment, but at least I had gotten the last shot. In the larger scheme of things, you could even say that I had managed to snatch a moral victory out of the rubble of . . . phooey.

This was turning out to be a very bad day for the Security Division.

Double Trouble

I ran with no particular destination in mind. My only thought was to get far away from Sally May and her rotten little cat. Oh, and from Drover too. The thought of spending another minute with the King of Slackers was almost as dreadful as the prospect of getting thrashed by Sally May's broom.

I mean, let's face it. Drover had dared to make an intelligent decision on the field of battle (he ran before things got out of hand), and . . . well, I didn't feel emotionally prepared to deal with that. Maybe later, but not now.

I ran south as fast as I could go and didn't slow down until I reached the underbrush along the creek. There the brush closed around me like a dark curtain, and I was able to stop and catch my breath. And . . . might as well be honest here . . . I was able to pout and feel sorry for myself.

Why not? Didn't I deserve a pity party? Of course I did. I not only deserved it, but I had nothing else to do for the next . . . however long it took for Sally May to get over her latest Volcanic Moment.

Boy, it sure didn't take much to get her on the warpath. And what really broke my heart was that I had tried SO HARD to please her. Oh well.

I was in the midst of feeling sorry for myself when my thoughts were interrupted by . . . what was that? A voice? Yes, unless my ears were playing tricks on me, I had heard a voice coming from the other side of the curtain of brush, perhaps from the creek.

And here's what the voice said: "Now, Momma, just try to stay calm. I'll talk to 'em, and we'll get everything straightened out."

Then another voice said, "Freddy, you can't talk to a wolf!"

"Momma, I'll handle it. You just be still, hear?"

You know, there was something familiar about those voices, and did you notice the names they used? Momma and Freddy. Hadn't I run into somebody named . . .

Wait, hold everything! You probably missed the clues, but I didn't. It was those birds again, the pelicans! I had given them strict orders to leave my ranch, but they were still hanging around. And they were fixing to feel the wrath of the Security Division. By George, I'd taken my lumps from the cat, but I didn't have to take trash off a couple of skinny-legged pelicans.

I plowed my way through the wall of brush and burst out into the clearing, and there they were, two ridiculous birds standing out in the middle of the creek.

I announced my presence in a loud voice. "Hank the Cowdog, Special Crimes. You're all under arrest! Freeze, nobody moves!"

Heh heh. That gave 'em a scare. When I announce myself in that voice, it always gets their attention. To tell you the truth, it's kind of fun to go busting into the middle of somebody's party; and believe me, those birds were shocked.

After a moment of dead silence, Momma said, "It's that dog again."

Freddy swallowed a lump in his throat. "Momma, be still, I'll do the talking."

I marched up to the water's edge. "Freddy, I thought I told you to clear out of here."

"Yes sir, we tried; but you know, I think we

just flew in a big circle and Momma was getting tired and, well, here we are again. We was kind of hoping you wouldn't notice."

"How foolish of you. Fishing? Is that what we have here, fishing without a license, without permission? It's called trespassing, and you're in big trouble."

"Yes, well, we've got other troubles too."

I noticed that Freddy was doing something with his eyes, jerking them toward the south, and one of his wing tips seemed to be pointing in the same direction. I let my gaze drift to the south and . . . uh-oh.

Okay, remember that Momma said something about "a wolf"? I hadn't paid much attention to it at the time, and all at once I wished I had, because . . . you'll never guess who or whom I saw standing on the opposite side of the creek.

Here's a couple of hints: big dudes, scruffy, large spiky teeth, and glittering yellow eyes.

Holy smokes, it was Rip and Snort, the cannibal brothers! They were standing on the other side of the creek, tuning up for a song. No kidding. You might remember that they had terrible voices but loved to sing. You want to hear it? Okay, brace yourself.

Cannibal Trash

I guess you think we ain't wonderful singers.
You might even think that we can't rhyme
verses.
Well, maybe we can't, and we really don't care.
We sing what we want and beat up our critics.

And now that you know about cannibal music,
You'd better shut up and listen real good.
'Cause some of you think that we're pretty
rude guys,
But down where it counts . . . you're right; we
are rude.

Trash, trash, cannibal trash.
And if you don't like it, we'll give you a
bash.
Our smell is so awful, it causes a rash.
We're proud to announce that we're
cannibal trash.

The wimmen all love us and think we are cool.
We learned all our manners at cannibal
school.
They love our aroma and deep, manly odor.
The fragrance of skunk is the gas in our
motor.

I bet this song has opened your eyes,
'Cause now you know we're the coolest of
guys.
So tune up your tonsils and join in our noise.
Just sing like a couple of junior high boys.

Trash, trash, cannibal trash.
And if you don't like it, we'll give you a
bash.
Our smell is so awful, it causes a rash.
We're proud to announce, really proud to
announce,
We're proud to announce that we're
cannibal trash.

Well, what can you say? Rip and Snort had always been drawn to trashy songs, and this one sure proved it. But what worried me was that after they finished the song, they pointed toward the pelicans and started licking their chops.

I lowered my voice to an urgent whisper. "Hey, Freddy, you've got a serious problem—two of them, in fact."

He nodded. "Right. I was fixing to talk to 'em when you popped out of the brush." He leaned toward me and lowered his voice. "They look kind of hungry, don't they?"

"They're always hungry... and very dangerous. I know them pretty well."

"You don't reckon they'd eat a pelican, do you?"

"I think I know the answer, but let me check." I turned to the brothers and forced up a pleasant smile. "Hey, Rip, Snort! How's it going, fellas?"

Snort gave me a sour look. "Fellas going hungry."

"Yes, well, at the end of the day, we're all working for our stomachs, aren't we? Ha ha." They didn't laugh or even smile. "Say, this weather's been nice, hasn't it?" No response. "Hey, how's the family? Kids are growing up, I guess." Dead silence. "You know, it's hard to carry on a conversation with someone who doesn't talk."

"Rip and Snort not give a hoot for conservation. Ready to eat two gooses." He pointed toward Freddy and his mother.

"Snort, they're not geese."

"Gooses."

"They're not gooses either. They're pelicans from the Gulf of Mexico, and they just popped in for a little visit. I gave them permission to swim in my creek, don't you see, and, well, here they are. In other words, we have some guests from out of town, and I'm sure you'll agree that we shouldn't go around eating our guests."

The brothers roared with irreverent laughter.

I turned to Freddy. "You need to get out of here."

He pulled his chin and wagged his head. "Well, I hear what you're saying, but Momma's worn plumb out, and she's got authoritis in her shoulder."

I leaned out toward him. "Hey, Freddy, if those coyotes decide to eat you, which they *will,* your momma won't have to worry about her shoulder because there won't be anything left of her but feathers. You need to leave, real quick."

"Well, let me see what she says." He turned to his mother. "Momma, Hank thinks we need to move along."

She shot me a hot glare. "Is he the one that called me an old fossil? You tell him to stick his head in a bucket of grease! I'm tired, and I ain't moving."

Freddy turned back to me. "She's feeling a little crabby right now. Maybe you could talk to her."

"Me? Hey, pal, we tried that once and I've still got knots on my head. Remember that?"

He rocked up and down on his toes. "She's pretty set in her ways, all right."

This looked hopeless. Those birds had no more common sense than a chicken . . . and why was I even trying to help them? I couldn't think of a single reason, not one. Thoughts swirled through my mind, then...

"Wait. I've got an idea. Pelicans catch fish, right?"

"Oh yeah, we're good fishers." A dreamy smile swept over his beak. "Did I ever tell you about the time I scooped up a barracuda? Big rascal and, boy, you talk about bite!"

"Freddy, hush. Concentrate. Catch a fish. Now."

"Now? Well, I guess I could try. Let me see what I can find."

He looked down into the creek, walked a few steps, and drove his snoot into the water. When his beak came up again... my goodness, the lower part had become a kind of basket, and it seemed to have something flopping around inside.

Freddy beamed with pride and spoke with his mouth full. "I got one!"

"Great. Hang onto it." I turned toward the coyote brothers. "Hey, guys, I've got some great news. How do you feel about fresh fish?"

The brothers exchanged puzzled looks. "Not feel nothing for fretch fitch. Not give a hoot for fretch fitch."

"Actually, Snort, fish is very good for you. It's low in fat and high in all that other stuff that's good for you: vitamins and minerals, protoplasm, ectoplasm—all the good stuff."

"Ha. Coyote not give a hoot about vallamins and miserables. Coyote only care about MEAT!"

I turned to Freddy. "Throw the fish up on the bank, and we'll see what they do."

Freddy nodded and whipped his beak around, flinging a nice big catfish onto the bank in front of the brotherhood. The fish flopped around in front of them. Snort moved closer and took a sniff.

"Uh. Fretch fitch stink."

I had to think fast. "Well, of course it stinks, and that's what makes it the perfect coyote food. You guys stink, right?"

The brothers traded grins. "Ha! Brothers stink pretty good and proud of it too!"

"Well, there you go. You'll love fish, give it a try."

Snort grumbled something under his breath and eased his nose toward the fish. He licked his chops and opened his bear trap jaws and...BLAP! The fish smacked him across the chops.

Snort beamed me a ferocious glare. "Stupid fretch fitch slap Snort face!"

"Well, it's a fish, what do you expect? Just bull your way through and gobble it down."

Snort glared down at the fish. "Dummy not get

away from Snort, ho ho." The bear trap opened wide; Snort scooped up the fish and slammed his jaws shut. He grinned and started chewing. Suddenly his eyes popped wide-open. He stopped chewing and spit the fish out on the bank. "Fretch fitch sting Snort mouth!"

Oops. I had forgotten that catfish have sharp fins on their backs and sides, and when they stab something, it hurts.

Well, Snort was mad now. He pounded his chest and roared, "Rip and Snort not waste time with dummy fretch fitch! Ready to eat goose, oh, boy!"

I whirled back to Freddy. "That's it, pal, I'm out of ideas. When they start saying 'Oh, boy,' it means they're ready to eat. You need to leave. Hurry, fly up into one of those trees."

Freddy's face settled into a mournful look. "Momma hates trees. They hurt her feet."

I dashed out into the water and screamed in his face. "You're thinking about her feet? Idiot! Those guys are cannibals, and they're fixing to eat you! Get out of here; fly away!"

He flinched. "Well, let me talk to Momma."

Over on the south bank, Rip and Snort were going through their normal warm-up procedures—pounding their chests, roaring, pawing up dirt, and butting their heads against trees. It sent shivers down my spine, but do you suppose the dingbat pelicans showed the slightest concern?

None. Zero. I stared in amazement as they stood there in the middle of the creek—kind, patient Freddy trying to talk sense to his mother, who stood like a statue with her wings folded across her chest. She was listening but hearing nothing.

And time was running out. Oh well, I had tried to help. Sometimes we can save the helpless, and sometimes they become stastisticks . . . stustisticks . . . phooey. Some of them become snacks for cannibals. There wasn't a thing I could do to help.

Just as I had feared, Rip and Snort finished their warm-ups and turned their fearsome yellow eyes toward the birds. They swept long, red tongues across their mouths and then...

Here they came, pounding through the shallow water like racehorses, sending a spray of water flying in all directions. Helpless on the north bank, I could only watch the massacre unfoil. I had a feeling that it would be a pretty short massacre.

Snort got there first. His jaws were wide-open, his shark teeth gleaming in the afternoon sun. I cringed, waiting to hear... I didn't even want to think about it.

WHOP

WHOP!

Huh? Remember that Momma Pelican was "worn plumb out" and had arthritis in her shoulder? Well, she got over it. In a flash, she cocked back her wing and gave Snort a whack across the nose that almost sent his head underwater. Then she squawked, "You nasty old thing, don't you be making teeth at me!"

Freddy patted her on the shoulder. "Now, Momma, please be careful. They don't act hardly normal."

Yipes, there was fire in Snort's eyes, and we're not talking about a little fire. It was the kind of fire that says, "This goose is fixing to be cooked!"

When Momma saw that look of pure meanness, she let out a gasp and grabbed hold of her son. "Freddy, do something!"

Freddy's eyes went blank and he froze.

Justice Triumphs Again!

Well, what's a dog supposed to do, sit there and watch while a couple of bird-brained tourists get mugged by the local cannibals? I didn't want to get involved, but I had no choice.

I grabbed a gulp of air and dived into the water, went bounding out into the middle of the creek, and took aim at a set of tail feathers. CHOMP! Feathers flew and so did Momma.

Freddy's mouth dropped open. "You bit my momma!"

"And you're next, unless you get out of here! Fly, fly, fly!"

Glory be, he finally figured it out and flapped up into the sky. At that point, I turned to face . . . gulp . . . two ferocious dragons. I mean, I had more or less spoiled their supper plans, and they appeared to be REALLY MAD about it. Clearly, this would be a test of my diplomatic skills.

I molded my face into a friendly smile. "Guys, I know what you're thinking, but if you'll give me a moment, I think I can explain everything, no kidding." They kept creeping toward me, their eyes crackling with unholy light. I began easing backward toward the north bank. "Snort, let me remind you that those birds were pelicans, not geese; and it's common knowledge that pelican meat is, well, tough and stringy. Very tough. You'd have been disappointed, honest."

They kept coming. You know, when coyotes stop talking, it's usually a bad sign. Okay, charm wasn't going to bail me out of this deal. I would have to rely on my amazing speed and quickness.

In the blink of an eye, I whirled around, pointed myself to the north, and pushed the throttle lever all the way to Turbo Seven. The roar of rocket engines filled the air, and the world whizzed past me in a blur. Huge trees bent to the ground. Dust swirled behind me. Ants scampered into their holes, and butterflies flapped and fluttered to get out of my...

BAM!

Huh? I was lying in the sand on the north bank

of the creek. I looked up and saw what appeared to be a tree towering over me, only it had hair and sharp teeth and looked a lot like an angry coyote.

"Snort? Hey, you were out in the middle of the creek just a second ago. How did you..."

His jagged laughter sent chills down my spine. "Hunk slower than turtle and dumber than goose. Now Rip and Snort make supper out of Hunk, ho ho!"

"Hey, it's too early for supper. Snort, could we discuss this? Don't forget that dogs and coyotes are distant cousins. Snort?"

Imagine that you're standing onstage, looking out at a huge auditorium full of TEETH. That's what I saw when Snort opened his mouth.

Well, I'd had a pretty good life—a few victories, a few defeats, and a few laughs in between. I wasn't quite ready to check out, but it appeared... gulp... that we were getting close to the end.

But suddenly . . . you won't believe this . . . at the very last second, something strange happened. An unidentified object dropped out of the sky and struck Snort on top of the head with a loud splattering sound.

He closed his jaws and rubbed his head and turned to his brother. "Uh. Something smack Snort on top of head." Rip nodded and pointed toward a strange object that was flopping around on the creek bank. Snort looked closer and grunted, "Uh! Fretch fitch fall out of sky?"

Rip thought that was pretty funny and started laughing . . . until he heard an odd whistling sound overhead. He raised his eyes . . . just in time to catch a two-pound bass right on the end of his nose. BLAP!

At that point, the brothers weren't laughing. Their eyes grew wide, and they began looking around in all directions. While Rip rubbed his nose, Snort muttered, "Uh! Fretch fitch raining down from overhead sky!"

Rip nodded and said, "Uh!"

Snort gave his head a vigorous shake and roared, "Snort not believe in raining fretch fitch from sky! Must be some kind of phooey trick!" BLAP! A three-pound catfish came streaking out of the sky and beaned him so hard, it knocked him to his knees. He pushed himself up on wobbly legs and grunted. "Uh. Maybe Snort believe in raining down fretch fitch."

BAM! This one was a five-pound carp, and it landed right between the brothers. Snort stared at the carp. "Uh. Fretch fitch big enough to put big hurt on coyote brothers." Rip nodded and began backing away. Snort began backing away.

BAM! Another big carp rained down from the sky, missing Snort by only a matter of inches.

That did it. Snort didn't know what was going on, but he wanted no more of it. In a flash, two full-grown coyotes vanished and went crashing through the brush along the creek.

Well! That was pretty interesting, all those fish falling out of the sky; and they had certainly come at a good time for me. I mean, one more minute and I would have been crow bait.

But what had caused the sky to rain down fish? It was one of the strangest events I'd seen in my whole career. I was in the process of trying to figure it out when I heard a PLOP behind me. I whirled around and saw...

You probably think it was another fish, right? Well, you're wrong. What I saw wasn't another fish but *a big bird wearing a silly grin*. Freddy. And all at once, the pieces of the peezle began falling into a puddle.

All the pieces of the puzzle began falling into place, let us say.

I stared at him in disbelief. "You did this?"

"Yeah, me and Momma. It was her idea, but I done the biggest part of the work." He chuckled and gave me a wink. "Back home they call me the Brownsville Bomber."

"Yes, I can see why. You're pretty good."

That made him proud. "Thanks. It ain't over 'til the fat lady gets hit by a fish while she's singing."

"Amazing! Well, Freddy, I hardly know what to say... except thank you. You really saved my hide on that one."

"Well, you kind of saved ours too." His face grew solemn. "But Hank, I've got some bad news. Brace yourself." He moved closer and laid a wing on my shoulder. "We're gonna leave."

My heart leaped for joy. "Freddy, that's... that's awful news! You can't stick around for another month or two?"

He wagged his head and pointed a wing toward the sky, where his mother was flying around in a holding pattern. "Nope. Momma's made up her mind; she wants to go home."

"Do you think you can find your way back?"

He gave his head a solemn nod. "I think I figured it out. The Gulf's south of here, so if we fly *south,* we'll find it."

"Freddy, that's brilliant." I shook his hand . . . wing. "Well, I wish you a safe trip. Say hello to all the jellyfish."

He grinned and whispered behind his wing, "Say, did I ever tell you about the time I scooped up a big old jellyfish in my beak? Heh. Those things have stingers, don't you know, and..."

Overhead, Freddy's mother screeched, "Freddy, come on, we're a-burning daylight!"

He shrugged. "I guess I'd better go."

"Freddy, I have two small favors to ask. First, tell your mother I'm sorry I called her an old fossil."

He nodded. "That's nice, she'll be happy to hear it." He glanced over each shoulder and whispered, "But you know, she does kind of look like one, don't she?" We shared a laugh. "What was the second favor?"

"The second thing is . . . before you fly south, I would really appreciate it if you would . . ." I whispered my request.

You're probably dying to know what I said, but I'm not going to tell you. You'll just have to keep reading.

Well, we said our good-byes, and Freddy launched himself back into the sky. I made my way back to ranch headquarters and went straight to the yard fence. Guess who was still sitting on the porch, purring and staring out at the world with weird eyes. Mister Kitty Precious.

When he saw me at the gate, his face burst into a gleeful expression. "Oh goodie, it's Hankie again! What brings you back to the scene of your most recent disgrace?" He snickered.

"Pete, you're not going to believe this, but I've come to make peace."

"You're right, Hankie. I don't believe it. I've heard this before."

"I know, but this time it's different. All this bad blood between us . . . Pete, it's just not right. Think of all the years we've wasted, fussing and fighting."

"I know, Hankie, but it's been so much fun."

"Fun for you, not for me. I've had enough. Let's talk peace treaty."

Taking his sweet time, he came halfway down the sidewalk and stopped. He turned and glanced back at the house. It was then that I noticed . . . oops . . . Sally May's face framed in the kitchen window. Don't forget that she had Radar for Naughty Thoughts, and she had her antenna aimed straight at me.

Sally May's looming presence seemed to give Kitty a rush of courage, and he came prancing the rest of the way to the gate. He curled his tail around himself, sat down, and flashed a crazy smile.

"Hankie, it doesn't matter whether we make

war or peace—*you always lose*. It's just a fact of nature. It happens every time."

"I'm willing to take the chance, Pete, because, well, I believe in miracles."

"Really! How interesting." He licked his paw. "I don't."

"Okay, what would you say if a fish fell out of the sky? Would that be a miracle?"

WHAP! A perch hit the ground beside him. Kitty went off like a loaded mousetrap, jumped two feet straight up in the air. It was hilarious, but I kept a straight face.

Pete stared at the fish, then turned a glare on me. The wheels in his mind were turning. "What are you up to, Hankie?"

"Was it a miracle or not?"

"It won't happen again in a thousand years."

BLAP!

This time Freddy nailed him, and you never saw a cat jump higher in the air. We're talking about five feet straight up, like a little spring that had been pinched down and then released. Oh, and he cut loose with a delicious squeal. "Reeeeeeeer!"

"What do you say now, Pete? Do you believe in miracles?"

For once in his life, Kitty was speechless. This

had blown his tiny mind. He had no idea what was going on, and he didn't stick around to talk about it. In a flash, he was gone.

I loved it, absolutely loved it. But then... uh-oh ... seconds later, the back door burst open and out came Sally May, pumping her arms the way she does when she's mad.

"All right, Hank, I've had about enough of..."

BLAP! Another fish hit the grass. Sally May froze in her tracks... looked at the fish, looked at me, looked up in the sky... and ran back inside the house!

Ho! This was almost too good, even better than I had dared to hope. By George, we had bombed the cat and... BLAP!

Huh? Good grief, Freddy was bombing ME!

"Hey, Freddy, you can call off the..." BLAP!

Well, the Brownsville Bomber appeared to be having a big time up there. He'd bombed two coyotes, one cat, the owner's wife, and even the Head of Security. For the next five minutes, no one on the ranch was safe.

It takes a while to motivate a pelican, but once you get 'em started, it's hard to shut 'em down.

Oh well, the impointant pork is that I had solved one of the most puzzling cases of my whole career and had saved a couple of clueless birds

from a terrible fate. Best of all, I had managed to get them off my ranch and out of my hair.

No, wait. Best of all was that I had finally managed to score a major victory against the little creep of a cat; and fellers, that was sweet. SWEET! Pete didn't come out of hiding for two days, and guess who got all his scraps. Hee hee. Best scraps I ever ate.

Wow, what a day! Slow start but a strong finish, which just goes to prove that it's always darkest before it gets any darker, so we should never give up hope.

And with that piece of wisdom, this case is closed.

Oh, one more thing. The people on my ranch never figured out how all those fish got in the yard. I mean, we're talking about seriously confused. Hee hee. You and I know the answer, but we're not talking.

Shh.

Have you read all of Hank's adventures?

1 *The Original Adventures of Hank the Cowdog*
2 *The Further Adventures of Hank the Cowdog*
3 *It's a Dog's Life*
4 *Murder in the Middle Pasture*
5 *Faded Love*
6 *Let Sleeping Dogs Lie*
7 *The Curse of the Incredible Priceless Corncob*
8 *The Case of the One-Eyed Killer Stud Horse*
9 *The Case of the Halloween Ghost*
10 *Every Dog Has His Day*
11 *Lost in the Dark Unchanted Forest*
12 *The Case of the Fiddle-Playing Fox*
13 *The Wounded Buzzard on Christmas Eve*
14 *Hank the Cowdog and Monkey Business*
15 *The Case of the Missing Cat*
16 *Lost in the Blinded Blizzard*

17 *The Case of the Car-Barkaholic Dog*
18 *The Case of the Hooking Bull*
19 *The Case of the Midnight Rustler*
20 *The Phantom in the Mirror*
21 *The Case of the Vampire Cat*
22 *The Case of the Double Bumblebee Sting*
23 *Moonlight Madness*
24 *The Case of the Black-Hooded Hangmans*
25 *The Case of the Swirling Killer Tornado*
26 *The Case of the Kidnapped Collie*
27 *The Case of the Night-Stalking Bone Monster*
28 *The Mopwater Files*
29 *The Case of the Vampire Vacuum Sweeper*
30 *The Case of the Haystack Kitties*
31 *The Case of the Vanishing Fishhook*
32 *The Garbage Monster from Outer Space*
33 *The Case of the Measled Cowboy*
34 *Slim's Good-bye*
35 *The Case of the Saddle House Robbery*
36 *The Case of the Raging Rottweiler*
37 *The Case of the Deadly Ha-Ha Game*
38 *The Fling*
39 *The Secret Laundry Monster Files*
40 *The Case of the Missing Bird Dog*
41 *The Case of the Shipwrecked Tree*
42 *The Case of the Burrowing Robot*
43 *The Case of the Twisted Kitty*
44 *The Dungeon of Doom*
45 *The Case of the Falling Sky*
46 *The Case of the Tricky Trap*
47 *The Case of the Tender Cheeping Chickies*
48 *The Case of the Monkey Burglar*

The following activities are samples from *The Hank Times,* the official newspaper of Hank's Security Force. Do not write on these pages unless this is your book. Even then, why not just find a scrap of paper?

For more games and activities like these,
be sure to check out Hank's official website at
www.hankthecowdog.com!

Rhyme Time

If Slim decides it's time to give up the cowboy life and leave the ranch, what kind of job could he find to do?

Make a rhyme using SLIM that would relate to his new job possibilities.

Example: Slim becomes a musical director at a church and leads the singing of songs:
SLIM'S HYMNS

1. Slim invents a switch that allows you to make the lights a little less bright.

2. Slim makes the metal ring that you put a basketball net on.

3. Slim opens a barbershop.

4. Slim gets a job cleaning leaves out of a swimming pool.

5. Slim opens a coffee shop known for filling your cup to the very top.

6. Slim starts a tree trimming business.

7. Slim opens a fitness club where people come to exercise.

8. Slim gets a job pointing out the winner in a race, saying "It's ____."

9. Slim comes up with a new diet drink that helps you lose weight.

10. Slim moves to California and becomes a beach lifeguard.

ANSWERS

1. SLIM DIM
2. SLIM RIM
3. SLIM TRIM
4. SLIM SKIM
5. SLIM BRIM
6. SLIM LIMB
7. SLIM GYM
8. SLIM HIM
9. SLIM SLIM
10. SLIM SWIM

Tropical Illusion

These two drawings may look the same. However, my cowdog eye sees that it is just a "tropical" illusion. A "tropical" illusion is something that isn't what it appears to be. And these drawings may look the same, but they're not. Can you find the 11 differences between them?

Answers on last page of Security Force Activities

Security Decoding Information

	1	2	3	4	5	6
A	F	M	I	R	T	E
B	O	K	H	U	A	N
C	P	J	C	D	I	S

Use the decoder to unscramble a line that Drover was heard singing in the song "It's Not Smart to Show Your Hiney to a Bear."

"C5 A1 B3 A6 C2 B4 A2 C1 A6 C4

__ __ __ __ __ __ __ __ __ __

A3 B6 A5 B1 B1 B4 A4 C1 C5 C3 B2 B4 C1

__ __ __ __ __ __ __ __ __ __ __ __ __,

A3 C4 C2 B4 C6 A5 C3 A4 B1 B5 B2."

__'__ __ __ __ __ __ __ __ __ __."

ANSWER

"If he jumped into our pickup, I'd just croak."

Hank Quote

Unscramble the tiles below to reveal a line Hank sings in the song “Be a Winner.”

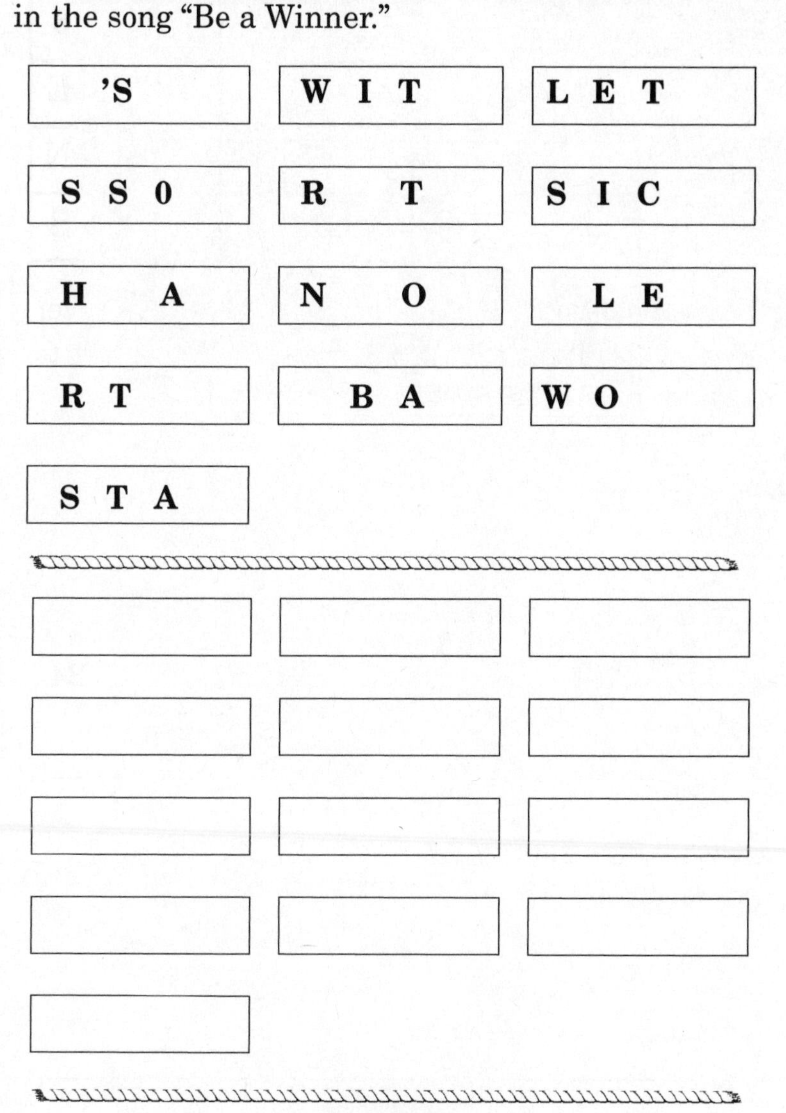

ANSWER

Let’s start with a basic lesson or two.

Tropical Illusion

Answer

Are you a big Hank the Cowdog fan? Then you'll want to join Hank's Security Force! Here is some of the neat stuff you will receive:

Welcome Package

- A Hank paperback
- An Original (19"x25") Hank Poster
- A Hank bookmark

Eight digital issues of *The Hank Times* with

- Lots of great games and puzzles
- Stories about Hank and his friends
- Special previews of future books
- Fun contests

More Security Force Benefits

- Special discounts on Hank books, audios, and more
- Special Members Only section on website

Total value of the Welcome Package and *The Hank Times* is $23.99. However, your two-year membership is **only $7.99** plus $5.00 for shipping and handling.

☐ Yes I want to join Hank's Security Force. Enclosed is $12.99 ($7.99 + $5.00 for shipping and handling) for my **two-year membership**. [Make check payable to Maverick Books.]

Which book would you like to receive in your Welcome Package? (#   ) any book except #50

BOY or GIRL

YOUR NAME (CIRCLE ONE)

MAILING ADDRESS

CITY STATE ZIP

TELEPHONE BIRTH DATE

E-MAIL (required for digital Hank Times)

Send check or money order for $12.99 to:

Hank's Security Force
Maverick Books
PO Box 549
Perryton, Texas 79070

DO NOT SEND CASH. NO CREDIT CARDS ACCEPTED.

Allow 2–3 weeks for delivery.

Offer is subject to change.

Photo Courtesy of Western Horseman Magazine

John R. Erickson, a former cowboy, has written numerous books for both children and adults and is best known for his acclaimed ***Hank the Cowdog*** series. He lives and works on his ranch in Perryton, Texas, with his family.

Gerald L. Holmes has illustrated numerous cartoons and textbooks in addition to the ***Hank the Cowdog*** series. He lives in Perryton, Texas.

Shawn Tevis Photography

Harris County Public Library
Houston, Texas

2